T0129238

House of Elliott

The Good Son

Mirthell Bayliss Bazemore

ISBN: 978-1-4669-6376-4 (sc)
ISBN: 978-1-4669-6375-7 (e)

Trafford rev. 12/03/2012

 www.trafford.com

North America & international
toll-free: 1 888 232 4444 (USA & Canada)
phone: 250 383 6864 ♦ fax: 812 355 4082

Dedicated to my mother

Euradell Bernice Bayliss

Lionel Bazemore

This book would not have been possible without the help of the extraordinary support of my husband Not only did he provide emotional support throughout my writing career, but sacrifice of time.

Jeanine Nicholas & Wendy Hsieh

It has been a pleasure and honor to share my story with you. Thank you for your encouragement, analysis and support with this story.

Sandie L. Bazemore

Always follow your dreams and heart desires. Thank you for your support and encouragement, love always—Mother.

Special thanks to my readers who have followed this trilogy and loved my characters:

IF I DIE, YOU DIE
THE UGLY SIDE OF BEAUTY
HOUSE OF ELLIOTT

This story is about deception, love, possession and revenge. A young man torn between four women who love him, yet all equally wicked in different ways. Raised by a woman that Frances presumed to be his mother, only to find out he was living a lie. The first thirty years of his life—He lived as Alex Bowles, when his true name is ~ Frances Elliott lll.

It has been said that "The truth is supposed to set you free". But for Frances, it was the beginning of more deception, lies and even murder.

Chapter One

(The Discovery)

Life for most people begins in the delivery room of a hospital or in the privacy of a bedroom at home with a midwife at hand. As for me, my beginning started at an automobile wreckage. Tossed in a lonely ditch waiting to die or be saved. This is my story and my beginning.

As an only child I had everything a child could want when it came to the material things. However, my mother was over protective, over bearing, very religious and simply paranoid about life. I grew up in an environment where if it didn't agree with her, then it was the work of the devil. Nevertheless, I loved her still and she loved me. But having both parents and siblings was what I wanted most of all. I did not like being an only child, which left me alone most of the time. I enjoyed the family dynamic. My mother told me that my father was killed in the Gulf War before I was born. There were no pictures of him, unless she kept them in a secret place. Whenever I asked her about my father and his pictures, she was uncomfortable and didn't like talking about him. She said her anger and pain caused her to destroy his pictures. I believed her; until the day I found out she lied.

It is sad when haunting lies end, and there is nothing you can do to stop it. It is like a volcano erupting and destroying everything in its path. Nothing seems to makes sense to me anymore and her lies have finally caught up with her; unraveling, to say the least—as if a thread of yarn has been pulled from various directions. I hear the sound of her cries, and yelling for me to not leave her alone as I walked out of her life. It will haunt me forever as much as this new known truth I have just discovered. A woman I once loved and called my mother is dying. I am walking out of the door before she takes her last breath. Knowing there is a level of conscience in her mind. This may sound heartless and evil of me, but my life has been plagued by evil and deception. I do not even know who I am; my life is not even mine. How could it be? It has been one big lie. My mother named me Alex Bowles, but my true name is Frances Elliott.

I lived in a small town called Hampton near England, with my mother Alexandria Bowles. It was a peaceful quiet town where you knew your neighbors, and everyone seem to get along. We were happy even though we did not have a traditional family. My mother was very strict and did not like me having too many friends. She felt too many friends would hinder my education and religious belief. This was strange because our community was family oriented, predominately catholic, and quite friendly. I guess she felt they would ask questions about my father, or pry into our personal business and she was very secretive. At times we kept to ourselves until the neighbor's daughter Cathy and her twin brother Carlton would come and visit with me. We became friends at a young age and we grew up together. She was my neighbor and one true friend. I could confide in her about anything. She was genteel, sweet and beautiful. Cathy had long, dark wavy hair and her skin was very fair with rosy cheeks. She had the prettiest grey eyes and a curvy figure. Always very thoughtful and I treated her as if she were my sister, though I felt our feelings for each other were changing as we got older. She had a crush on me since I was a kid, and I had a crush on her as well. Cathy really liked my mother and enjoyed having bible study with her from time to time. I use to love when she had dinner with us, which was often. Some of the neighbors use to say my mother's behavior was odd, because she was somewhat of a recluse. Cathy never felt that way about her and always saw the good in her. Cathy and I had thought that my mother's strange behavior was due to my father's sudden death, due to war—Depression. However, no! I would find out later it was fear. Fear of being caught for child abduction and fleeing from an accident scene. You see, my mother was driving home from work one Christmas Eve. She was not too far from her home when she heard a car accident. When she went to investigate the scene, she heard a baby crying in the bushes. Instead of doing the right thing by assisting the victims and waiting for the paramedics to arrive, she took the baby and fled the scene. She would then claim the child to be her own—I was that baby. She was right about her husband being killed in the war. However; wrong about ever bearing his child. So, the question I have is—who am I? I know Frances Elliott was my father, but who am I? Who is my real mother? Are my natural parents still alive? Do I have a family that I do not even know? All these questions plagued my mind and eventually destroyed my relationship with the woman I called mother.

The thought of someone suffering a horrible car accident, and loss of a child after losing her spouse is incomprehensible. How could a woman be so cruel and selfish, during a time when someone else was suffering badly?

Everything became known when my mother Alexandria, was diagnosed with cancer of the pancreas six months ago. Though she tried to fight it, this illness overcame her and there was nothing I can do to ease her pain; and her suffering was killing me as well. She was all I had! As her cancer had progressed she required higher dosages of morphine, which would dull her pain and act as a truth serum. She would tell me how much she loved me, wanted me to read scriptures to her. How much she loved Cathy and felt we should marry. Whatever was in her heart to say, she said. I was her care provider along with Cathy. She would bathe her, cook for her and help with laundry. One day after giving her morphine, she started having a fit asking for her diary box. Not sure why she wanted it, I gave it to her to calm her down. She held it tight as if it were a treasure box close to her heart. I sat next to her reading her favorite scripture—*The Great Invitation: Matthew 11:28-30,* while Cathy held her hand. Her voice was weak and broken at times, but she kept saying, "I should have saved them all". As soon as she fell asleep and Cathy left the room. I pried the dairy from her hands and a newspaper clipping fell from it. What I saw would be the volcano erupting in my life. It was a newspaper clipping with a picture of a family, and obituary. The picture on the obituary was a mirror image of my face. It read "Frances Elliott II Killed in Car Crash & Infant son missing". I was mortified because the face of Frances was identical to mine, with the exception of my long shoulder length hair. While my mother slept I took the article to my room and sat at the edge of my bed. It was raining profusely that night and I felt a grim sickness coming over me. For a moment I just stared at the face of this man thinking, "This cannot be." My mother is dying, and there are questions to be answered. Not sure as to what to do, I just held the article in my hand and began to read it.

The article stated a man was driving home on Christmas Eve, with his family then loss control of his car and was killed. Survivors were a wife and two daughters. However, the husband had died and the infant baby boy was missing. The wife went mad at the scene and kept crying for her son, but he was never found. Search teams went out to search the area but no child was found. The wife stated that the baby was ejected from her arms upon impact. After several days of searching for the baby boy Frances Elliott III, he was also presumed dead.

The mother of the child posted pictures a week later of the baby with a reward, but there were no response. The mother feared her son was taken by some type of wild animal. Funny, how the mother assumed only a wild animal would do such an evil deed. Should I compare my mother to a wild animal?

After reading this article, I became ill, confused, and had a bad feeling about this. Why would my mother hold such an article? Then moan, "I should have saved them all" Right away I knew I was connected to this family. But did not want to accept what was coming my way. How could she have done this? Was there more to this story? This cannot be happening. Then I reflected back on my life and remembered once, a conflicted story she told me about my father. When I was five, I asked her what happened to my dad and she said he was killed in a hunting accident. Then at seven, a teacher asked her about my father in front of me and she said he was killed while serving his country. I tried to go to sleep and rethink about this situation in the morning. But my sleep was vexed and I kept tossing and turning and having nightmares. Therefore, I got up and I went back to her room and stood at the doorway watching her sleep. Wondering? Am I the missing child—Frances Elliott III?

It would be the next morning when the questions would begin, finding out exactly who I am. Where did I come from? Is my biological mother still alive? So many questions I had, and my anger got the best of me. The next morning when my mother woke up, I had asked Cathy to come to our home while I left to go to the library. I felt if I started there, I could get some good research done before confronting her. I took the newspaper clipping and left. When I got to the library I checked the microfilm for that same clipping. I read the full page article of the story about the Elliott family. Perhaps this was a coincidence that I looked like him. However, in my heart, I knew this was not a coincidence. It talked about the father and how he came from America and was about to open a bed & breakfast called *The House of Elliott* just before the fatal accident. He had a young family and was hard working and well respected in his community. After reading the article I went to the police department to further my research. I pulled in front of the police department and hesitated for a moment. "Do I want to really do this; am I mentally prepared for what was coming my way?" My nerves got the best of me thinking what if the officer tells me this family exists and I am only miles from them? Or, what if he tells me they're all dead? All these scenarios were running through my mind, as I hesitated going into the office.

When I got there and walked into the very busy office, I met a receptionist named Mary. I walked up to her and told her I was doing some research on a missing person. She offered her assistance and was quite pleasant until she asked the name. I told her the Frances Elliott case. The office seemed to quiet down after I said that name. There was a gentlemen officer sitting nearby who looked over at me as I said the family name. He got up and told the receptionist he would assist me. After thanking Mary for her assistance, I walked over to the officer's desk and sat down. He introduced himself as Sheriff Cardone and then offered me tea or coffee. I took coffee, black no sugar, then he asked me "what do you know about the Elliott family?" His back was turned to me as he was stirring his coffee. The officer's reaction was somewhat intriguing regarding the family. I told him "I was researching the missing child, the baby boy Frances Elliott III".

The officer just smirked, rubbed his head, leaned back in his chair, and said, "There was never a child found as we searched to no end, and did not find a baby at all". He said, "Either some wild animal smelled blood from the accident, maybe a pack of wolves or something. Or, on the other hand, someone could have got there before our emergency unit did and took the child. However, that would be unlikely". Then I asked him "Why the baby was presumed dead, without evidence?" and the officer leaned close to me and said, "We searched endlessly and no baby was found, so perhaps the wolves took the child. There are a lot of wolves in the area, especially that time of the season". He went on about this was a horrible scene, and no one wants to consider the thought of a child being eaten by a wolf. Then, he told me that the locals do not like bringing the situation up as that was an upsetting time for everyone. He walked over to the window in his office and said, "Frances Elliott was well liked in the community and his wife was a stunning and beautiful woman. It was a terrible situation" So then I asked for the location of their home and that is when he became irritated, and said, "Let it go son. This is a closed case and anyways—who are you?" He thought I was a reporter or something. I told him I have an interest in the family and was trying to get to the truth about what happened. He told me he has to make a call to get more information that might be helpful, which I thought was a bit odd. After making his call and getting off the phone, he said "Alex, I'm sorry but this is a cold case and the person I thought may be able to help you was of no assistance at all. I wish there was more I could tell you, but truth of the matter is—this case is closed". "Well, thank you anyways sheriff, I will be in touch".

I shook my head and walked out angrily, not understanding what was going on. Whom did he call? So, I asked the locals around town about the family and location of "House of Elliott" and this one woman spoke highly of it. Stating it is now one of the most prestigious girls' preparatory schools. I said "school?" and the lady went on about the school's reputation in her proud British accent. Finally, she told me where the school was located and I set off to check this place out. I was thinking this has to be some mistake. After getting directions from the stranger, sure enough the school was right there. It was a beautiful mansion, with an extended dormitory. Also a black Iron Gate surrounded the whole school. It was a replica of a modern day castle, stunning and beautiful!

As I stood outside the gate just before entering, I was greeted by the head mistress, Ms. Chauntelle. She stood firm wearing her blue skirt suit with an emblem sealed E on the lapel. She was tall, blonde and svelte. She also had a proud demeanor about her and seemed somewhat snobbish. As I walked up the large, wide stairway, I asked her jokingly "Hello! Do you always greet your guest this way standing outside"? She smirked at first and asked, "How can I help you" in her British tone. I was thinking she was the person called by the sheriff, just by her demeanor and annoyance with me. I lied and said "I have a daughter that is fourteen and was looking for a good school for her". Nevertheless, she saw right through my lies and invited me into her office, as she was walking rather quickly. However, my eyes were wondering all over the place checking out the paintings on the wall and the grandeur of this building. She stood at her door with it opened and asked me to come in and have a seat. After having a seat, I was given a large brochure and folder of what the school was about and what it had to offer. Quite pricey indeed, nothing I could afford. However, I noticed there was a beautiful woman printed on the cover named Clarice, with three other women equally as beautiful as her listed as board members.

As I stared at the pictures on the brochure, all that I could think was, "Was that my mother and possibly my sisters? A hurt came over me, and then I was asked by Ms. Chauntelle, "Is there anything else I can help you with?" I thought for a second and then I asked for a tour. The woman looked at me, annoyed and said, "You would have to make an appointment for that. And right now I'm scheduled out by two weeks and you would have to come back then". I said "two weeks?"

She then handed me the price sheet for the school and an application. The price was astronomical! The cost for one year was extremely pricey which included residence and boarding. My eyes must have gotten big, because she got up quickly and said her time was precious and that I must leave now. I got up, held the brochures in my hands for a second. I looked at her contemptuously and walked out.

When I walked outside to snoop around for a moment, I saw nothing out of the ordinary and then a security guard grabbed me and asked if he could assist me with leaving. I told him no, I could leave on my own, just as I came on my own. Clearly, these people were protecting something. Time was of the essence and I knew I needed to get back home to Cathy and my mother. I was sure by now they both were worried and concerned about my whereabouts as well as they should be. Being that I did not get anywhere with my investigation, I knew now I was going to have to confront my dying mother, and get her side of the story.

Chapter Two

(Confronting mother)

I was heading back home, driving back down the winding road while listening to some classical music. This day seemed particularly dreary with overcast clouds and lightening. A chill came over me as it started to rain. I almost felt ill from my visit, maybe it was the stress of all that has happened with my mother's sickness, and discovering such an ugly truth. Or perhaps, it was because I knew I had to confront her. My mind was jaded and consumed with all these thoughts. Then all of a sudden a large deer ran across the road. My car spun out of control as I slammed onto my brakes. I almost hit a tree as my tires hydroplaned, causing me to hit the curve side ditch. I was inches away from the embankment near a cliff. I jumped out of the car and made sure all was okay, but then that cold chill came over me again. It was of pure evil, I looked around very frightened and thought about what really happened that night; how easily one could lose control of their vehicle and be killed in a car accident. I saw my life flash before my eyes, and realized how short life can be; in an instant you can be gone. After getting my bearings together, I left and proceeded to go home. At that moment, I had the realization that the Elliott child could have been taken by a wolf, seeing how this area is known for wolves and deer's. Unknowingly as I was driving, I noticed there was a car parked in the woods that had observed everything—a police car and the officer inside never came to assist me, he just sat there. I believe it was officer Cardone.

When I got home, my mother was sitting up in her bed very coherent, reading her bible. I looked at her and sighed for a moment. By the look of my face, she knew something was wrong. She asked me "Alex, are you okay? Is there anything I can do to make things better?" She had to have known her article was missing. Then I sat at the edge of her bed and told said "Mother, I read the article. And, I have even had gone and been by the town where everything had happened. I went to the sheriff's department and the House of Elliott". Her eyes got big and water filled like I have never seen before and she looked away and tears poured down her face. She said

"I love you Alex and always will!"

I said to her, "Even to the point of stealing me from my biological mother, Clarice?"

She wept and begged for my forgiveness, but I did not acknowledge her plea. Instead, rage had come over me because she did not even try to deny it. She became apologetic, desperate and pitiful all at the same time.

Cathy had been with her all day and had just left when I drove up. I needed to talk to her but couldn't. I was too ashamed of what my mother had done. I would have not known where to begin or where to start. But I called her anyway and asked her to come back to our home and she did. I gave Cathy a hug and told her that I was going to be leaving again for a while. Also, I needed her to continue to watch over my mother. Without hesitation she said she would, but she knew something was horribly wrong. I could see the look in her beautiful grey eyes. They were warm and compassionate towards me. Then Cathy said,

"It must be pretty bad for you to leave your mother at this stage of her life"

"It is very bad Cathy, One day I will tell you. But for now, I have to sort this thing out"

Cathy and I had been long time friends, and to tell the truth, I too was in love with her and often thought about marrying her. Now my life is upside down, and my heart has been shattered. I was feeling very confused, distrusting, and nothing made sense to me anymore. I just wanted to get away, leave, and figure all this out. I felt that my mother was so full of lies and morphine that she could not possibly tell me the truth now. Cathy did not deserve my silence on this matter, but I just did not have the heart or courage to tell her what I have found out. I felt this would have hurt her as well, because she loves us both . . .

I went back into my mother's room and I stood over her feeling very disgusted. The guilt was written all over her face. Then I asked her "Was the man in the picture of that article my father?"

"Yes Alex! That was your father and Clarice is your biological mother"

Then she dropped her head in shame and refused to answer any more of my questions. However, her silence and tears spoke volumes and was enough evidence for me. I told her "I will never forgive you for what you had done. You have just made your last days easy for me to deal with" I walked out, and slammed the door.

She wept and cried out, "But it was me who truly loved you!" But, I kept walking until she heard the bedroom door slam close. I went into my room, grabbed a bag, packed a few items of necessity, and left out the front door as she screamed "Alex! Please don't leave me! God gave you to me—You're all I have!"

That night I drove back to that town and the weather was severe. I got a hotel, and looked over the brochure that Ms. Chauntelle had given me. I noticed that most of the stockholders and board members lived in New York. Clarice was president of the board and I assumed she lived there also.

The next morning I set off to the House and parked down the road. This time of year is very foggy and today was no exception. I walked about half a mile, hoping I could find an opening so I could really get in there. The place was well guarded so I had to wait for an opportune moment to get in, and I did just that. I waited for the early morning shift change and that is when I climbed the fence and was on the other side. I went in the back of the mansion and a vicious guard dog was in my midst and chased me further out behind the school. As I ran further towards the house, the dog just stopped due to another smaller fence. I kept going and saw an old rickety mansion a short distant ahead. It also had a gate around it; and an old broken down sign that read

"House of Elliott Bed and Breakfast"

Being that I was out of breath from all the running, I rested against a tall tree and proceeded to walk toward the house. The stairs were built to perfection as if the person took great pride in his masonry work. I broke the window beside the door, unlocked it, and then walked in. I was standing in the spider-webbed foyer looking around and there I saw old bloodstains on the floor. I felt such a strong spiritual presence here and the house was extremely cold. I could not believe I was here, in the place where my father once stood and built with his own hands according to the article. There was a huge, old painting of a man and his wife, my parents I suspected. As I wiped away the dust from their face, it was as if I was staring into a mirror. I dropped my head with disgust thinking why did this happen to me? I continued to walk around the house looking around and noticing parts of this mansion were cleaned as if someone had occupied it. The master bedroom was clean as if someone had used it recently. The bedding was new and the bathroom was clean. This was very weird to me because that meant that someone was residing in this creepy old mansion from time to time. But who could be living here? I had seen enough and went outside, I was overwhelmed with feelings and I began to feel nauseous. I leaned against t an old big tree outside in the back. While leaning against the tree I saw two small objects in the distance. As I moved closer to the objects I could see that they were two headstones. One said Frances Sr and the other baby Frances. So, I grabbed a large piece of broken wood from the rotted fence and used it as a shovel to dig the baby grave open. In it were baby trinkets, like baby booties, toys and a baby blanket, but there was NO baby skeleton or remains. I was consumed by anger; I needed to get to America to continue my quest. There was a New York address on the brochure for the branch school in America and that is where I was heading to find my family.

I called Cathy and told her I was leaving out of the country for a couple of weeks. I could hear the astonishment and hurt in her voice. Then she was quiet for a second, and said "Alex, I am concerned because of your mother's condition. What if she dies while you are away? How could you leave at a time like this? Surely, you can forgive her for whatever it was she had done?" For a moment I became quiet and did not say a word. Then I said, "Once I get back Cathy, I would fill you in on all the details. Nevertheless, I cannot until I have all of the answers myself. You have to trust me on this and know that I love you."

I booked a flight for New York and was off. Once I landed in New York after my long flight, I checked into a hotel and got some much-needed rest. The next morning, I drove to a town not far from New York City where the House of Elliott School was located. Once I arrived in that suburban town, I checked into a bed and breakfast, which was quite costly. I could've bought Cathy a Coach bag or myself a brand new 13' television for the cost of one night.

That same day I drove to the school, which was a mansion identical to the school in Europe. The students wore navy blue suits with the letter E emblem on the upper right side lapel, and they seemed to be all on one accord. All the girls favored each other and were very attractive. These women were beautiful, blonde, tall, and svelte. These girls almost seemed like Stepford girls. As I entered the school, it had an old world charm to it. There was a painting of Clarice, and two other women that were equally beautiful.

As I was staring at the beautiful pictures, a lady walked up to me whose picture was also on the wall. She introduced herself to me as Shay, Clarice's granddaughter. She was as breath taking as her painting on the wall. I told her I wanted to make an appointment to see Clarice and she looked at me up and down as if she had already been expecting me. She had directed me to the office and I made an appointment to see Clarice later that evening. The receptionist asked for my phone number and told me that Clarice will be giving me a call at her convenience before we meet. She also stated that someone—a physician would be stopping by my place of stay this afternoon, to run some blood test on me. DNA no doubt! But I was more than willing to have this test taken, to prove that I was in fact an Elliott. I'm sure by now they have checked my background, to make sure I had no criminal record and whatever else they wanted to know about me.

The granddaughter was looking at me and checking me out, out of the corner of her eyes. She made it obvious, as I turned to her and smiled to catch her staring at me. She looked at me with this smirk on her face; she did not even bother to play it off. It was almost chilling, as if something was going to happen to me, then she excused herself.

Before meeting Clarice I wanted to make a few changes to my appearance to make myself more presentable. So, I went back into town where my stay was and went to the local hair salon for men. My hair was a little past shoulder length. So I had decided to change my hairstyle and try a short nuwave look, to give me that GQ look. When I got back to where I was staying, there was a gentleman in the lobby waiting for me. He was carrying a black bag which looked like a medical bag and introduced himself to me as Dr. Rhys. We both went into my room and he explained that he was here to take a blood and saliva sample, for DNA purpose and that he worked for E.L.C. I had no problem with complying and gave him the samples he requested. The next morning I got up early around 6:30am shaved, showered, put on my nicest suit, and waited for the call. After looking at myself in the mirror, I realized just how much I looked like Frances Sr. (mirror image to say the least). Now I know why Shay was staring at me, it was because of my hippy like appearance. I guess in her own way she was telling me "Before you meet with Clarice, you had better clean up a little."

At six o'clock my phone rang and it was Clarice. Her voice was proper with a slight British accent and very soft spoken. She told me a limousine would be picking me up at my bed and breakfast in 30 minutes. I was astonished to hear her beautiful dainty voice. It did not sound aged or warm, it sounded almost like a business call. Those 30 minutes were the longest minutes of my life, anticipating the meeting with a woman who I believe to be my mother. After travelling so far, I will have my answers about what happened and more importantly, to reunite with her. I called Cathy to pass the time because I was starting to feel anxious. I don't know why, but now I had the urge to confide in her about what happened. Maybe it was the distance, and I did not have to face her—face to face. I told Cathy what was about to transpire and she was shocked. Yet, at the same time I could hear the sadness in her voice. Then just before hanging up the phone she stated, "I know you're excited about meeting your mother Clarice, but you need to be here right now with the mother who raised you" I understood her concern and told her "once I get all the answers I needed, I would return". Then Cathy said, "Alex, it may be too late then, your mother may not have much time left" the doctor had just left and told Cathy it was anytime now. Her breathing became shallow and there is a rattling sound in her chest. Fluid had built up in her lungs—death rattle! I put the phone to my heart for a second and told her "I have to go, my ride is here".

Once I hung up the phone, I started to feel somewhat guilty for abandoning the woman who raised me.

The driver took me on a 20-minute ride to this beautiful country club in the mountains. As I walked into the restaurant, I was treated like royalty and taken to my table where Clarice was sitting. I approached her slowly, she turned around and said "Alex!" she stood up and gently gave me a hug and looked into my watered filled eyes, and she kissed me on my left cheek. I embraced her in my arms and said, "Clarice Elliott, finally, we meet."

She ordered a bottle of Dom and wanted to propose a toast as she smiled at me. She was so graceful and youthful looking. After the waiter had poured our champagne, she said tilting her glass towards me "To our reunion" and she sipped her champagne looking into my eyes, while tears filled hers. She then put her hands on top of mine and told me how much I looked like Frances Elliott, my father. I could see her face light up as she talked about him. She spent the first 45 minutes talking about my father, his family, and accomplishments. I barely said a word, as I was in awe with her. I could tell she really loved him and still misses him dearly. Like a student, I listened to every word she uttered about him. Then, sadness came over her when she got to the part of his sudden death. This is where I came in and she let my hand go. She said she looked for me in her time of despair and tragedy but could not find me. She said the police told her there was no way a baby could have survived the accident, and if did, the elements alone with all the wild animals would have killed me. It never occurred to her that someone would be so cruel as to steal her child. I reared back in my seat and explained how hurt I was to find out such a thing. Then she told me that it appears that I was at least well taken care of. Then she asked me about my life; my education, love interest and about the woman that raised me? More so, how has my relationship changed with my other mother knowing what evil she had done? These were all very good questions and I had to be watchful how I answered them. I did not want to hurt her feelings; after all I loved my alleged mother who raised me.

I told her "this whole situation has made me look at her in a different light, with little respect and disgust. She is dying and I cannot stand to even look at her, so I left in search of you". She smirked, and said, "Sometimes life has a way of correcting itself and avenging the unjust. Let us order our food now". She ordered for both of us; lobster, asparagus and brown rice. She told me this was her favorite meal. But I could tell she felt a little uneasy so I asked her "Are you going to be okay?" And she said, "I am feeling a bit nervous, this is all so unexpected being back with my son" and then she chuckled. Perhaps this was all too much for her to take in.

I could not get over how youthful she looked, as if she was in her thirties. After our food was brought to us she asked me "So Frances, where do we go from here? This is all so very bizarre" as she was cutting into her lobster. That question took me by surprise; I did not really know how to answer except for saying "Yes, this is very bizarre and somewhat awkward for me, but I would love to have a relationship with my mother". She looked at me and smiled and said "Anything's possible my son" I asked her about my siblings and she enjoyed talking about my two sisters and stated she would like me to come by the department store tomorrow "Niece's" to meet the girls; Lavern and Tranice. We continued to talk about our lives and she told me about her parents. How much she loved my father and how much he loved me. We talked for hours; until we were the last two in the restaurant—she really loved him.

After dinner and getting reacquainted with each other, our date was ending and she insisted on picking up the pricey tab. I walked over to her and pulled her chair for she could get up and she was even more stunning in stature. She stood at 5'10 in height and must have weighed about 135 lbs. Beautiful silver hair, cut in a cute short European style. "Now I know where I got my svelte physique from

"I said. She smiled and gave me a hug. We walked to the limousine together, and talked about my flight and Europe. She was telling me how much she loves it there and it will always be home for her. She was very pleasant and enjoyed talking to me. She really started to open up to me about everything, her life, career, and daughters and I enjoyed every second of it.

Once the limousine arrived at my bed and breakfast, she said "My driver will be here tomorrow to pick you up at 10:00am for brunch"

"Thank you, I will be looking forward to seeing you tomorrow"

We parted with a kiss on the cheek and the limousine drove away.

Once I got back to my room, I could not fall asleep. I was thinking about her, my mother and all that I have been denied. I could have gone to one of those Ivy League universities like my sisters and enjoyed my siblings. I could have done or been much more than what I am today—an accountant and Sunday school teacher. I tossed and turned all night in my sleep, thinking all that could have been.

The next morning when I got up I thought about calling home and checking on my mother, but pride would not let me. I wanted her to suffer a little longer before getting back to Europe. After meeting my biological mother Clarice, I now realized I missed so much and there were so many unanswered questions about me as a person. Just as I was thinking about these things, Cathy called.

When I picked up the phone her voice was broken and she was very hurt. "Alex, your mother is barely holding on so you need to return at once. Her breathing is so shallow and she is asking for you. I don't know how much longer she has" I dropped my head and told her "I will be returning in a couple of days and I will explain everything to you when I get back. In the meantime Cathy, do whatever is necessary to keep her alive". She hung up the phone abruptly in my face.

The host of the bed and breakfast named Ivan told me that a limousine had arrived for me. I left and drove off to Niece's and I was given the VIP tour of the store. Then I was escorted by security to the elevator to the 30th floor where the corporate office is located. When the doors opened, Clarice was standing there looking amazing, wearing a two piece red suite. She had been waiting patiently for my arrival.

She took me to meet my oldest sister Lavern at her office. Lavern was the Chief Operations Officer of Niece's. She looked just like Clarice, tall, beautiful and graceful. She walked over to me and gave me a hug with tears in her eyes and said, "It has been so long since I hugged my little brother" then she cried. We both had tears of joy in our eyes.

She then quickly asked me "Are you okay? And how has life been treating you?" However, before I could respond Clarice said, "We'll discuss all those things at brunch dear, I must introduce you to your other sister—Tranice" So Clarice and I walked to the other side of the floor to Tranice office where the sign on her door read Chief Executive Officer and President. Seconds later we were buzzed in her corner suite office with her skyline view, overlooking New York City. She was wearing a two piece navy blue Armani pants suite with bright red Prada stilettos. She was on the phone and gestured her finger up for us to wait. Not quite the reception I was expecting. I could tell right away just by listening to her conversation on the phone, she was a power hitter and a real corporate bitch. I felt bad for whoever she was talking to on the other line of that phone call. Nonetheless, was also gorgeous, glamorous and very executive like. Once she hung up the phone, she turned and looked at both of us, with one eyebrow up.

Clarice said, "Darling, this is your brother Alex or should I say Frances?" Tranice looked at me up and down, walked over to me, and gave me a firm handshake. "Welcome to New York Frances! Mother has told me so much about you this morning" "Thank you Tranice"

She was very professional and a little standoffish until Clarice said "Okay children, were having brunch at 10:45am today, so let's head off to the dining room". She looked at her mother and said, "You could have given me a better notice mother. I need to go and freshen up and I will meet you over there at the executive dining room—it was nice meeting you Frances". I then looked at Clarice and she looked at me and said, "let us head over there now and wait for the girls to join us".

When we arrived the table was setup elegantly for us. After we were seated, she asked, "So son, what do you think of your sister's so far?" I told her "my sisters are beautiful and she did an outstanding job with them". "Yes I do agree! Tranice is a graduate of Yale and her major was business and economics. Lavern graduated from NYU and her major was marketing and business. She also attended Julliard and is an outstanding pianist. I am most proud of my accomplished daughters" Then Lavern walked up and sat down with us. She put her hand on top of mine and said, "My heart is overwhelmed with joy, having my baby brother back with us" Clarice just sipped her tea looking at me. Then Tranice walked in and the atmosphere of the room changed, as if it were now a business luncheon. She responded "Our missing brother Frances; so mother, what does this all mean?" Clarice just smirked!

Tranice looked at Lavern skeptically and said "What? Did I say something wrong?" "You could try being more tactful Neicey"

It was cute seeing how the sisters interact with each other even though the two are very different,_though they look identical. This is what I was missing in my life, having a complete family. I then assured her this was a friendly visit and reunion with our mother. Tranice responded "Hmmm" and proceed to order her food first. What arrogance I thought to myself, and then I looked at Clarice so she can order her food as well.

Tranice had many questions, more like an interrogation. We all ordered our lunch, and while waiting, I answered all her questions. Where did I live, if I was married, had children, my education and did our mother bring me to New York? I answered each one of her questions as if I were being interviewed. I could tell Lavern was a little embarrassed about her sister's behavior towards me, but it was okay. I had nothing to hide and my agenda was innocent. Tranice partially ate her food, while I felt she was studying me. She sipped her tea and then got up and walked over to me and said, "Well, it was nice meeting with you and I hope you enjoy your stay". I stood up and said, "Thank you Tranice, Likewise it was a pleasure reuniting with you and Lavern. I hope to see you again very soon" then she said "mother we will chat later" I asked Lavern "did I offend her?" "Not even! She has a lot on her plate and had a meeting to attend". Then Lavern asked me "the woman who raised you Frances, will she be arrested?" I sighed then said "NO, she is quite ill right now, and in her last days of life, her justice will come quickly for this evil deed she has done in my life"

"Was she cruel to you?" "No, I really thought she was my mother until a few days ago". Clarice asked, "Is she dying and from what?" "Yes—from cancer"

Then they both said "if she was kind to you, why are you not there with her now?" I told them "because I want her to suffer and feel my pain, she robbed me of so much and mislead me my whole life". Lavern smirked and said, "Spoken like a true Elliott!" then she jest towards her mother and said,

"He used your favorite word—Suffer!"

Clarice looked at Lavern and said to me "I think you should be by her side. There is no need for revenge in this case. Sometimes karma comes in a way to avenge the innocent. And after all, that is the woman who raised you and I am sure you two have shared many wonderful moments together" I was surprised to hear her say that. It was as if something cold and distant came over her. She was hurt, angry and her emotions seemed disconnected. I thought "how could you possibly say that after all that has happened?" And without a second thought Clarice angrily said, "Look son, you need to leave—Go and be with her!" I looked at Lavern and she said, "Well, I better excuse myself and it was nice meeting you Alex, I mean Frances" then she hugged me and was about to leave until I said "Mother, have I offended you? I didn't mean to upset you"

"No, you have not offended me—I'm just upset about this whole situation. You've come so far and I'm hurt that this lady took you from me and for only a short time she will suffer you. I have suffered you for the last thirty years. It's not fair that she robbed me of my child and now she is dying". I can feel the blood rushing to my face as I saw tears of pain running down my mother's pretty face. Then she said, "We have done what you set out to do . . . reunite; I am not sure what more I can do for you. The world I live in is very complicated and very different from yours."

Hearing her say that to me made me become very frustrated. What about showing some motherly love? But these women were different; cold, and lacking compassion. Perhaps Lavern being a little more compassionate than Tranice and Clarice, but even she walked away. I became hurt, angry and said "I came all this way to meet you". She replied "and you did, we did meet each other and reunited but there is nothing more to accomplish here. There is a woman who need you right at this very moment—Go Frances and be with her".

She looked at me hurt and stoned faced and said "Alex, we are done. I have to leave now for another engagement" Then she took the check, signed it and said "I am sorry things happened the way it did in our lives, but many years have gone by and there is a woman who needs you. Life goes on and it clearly has for both of us". Then she walked over to me, gave me this chilling hug goodbye, and walked off. It was the type of hug that said farewell forever. I was upset and confused, so I walked up to her and asked her "why are you acting this way towards me? Don't you see I love you and need you in my life?" She touched my face and said "Go on with your life son, I have" and walked out. When I walked out of the building the limousine was there and waiting to take me back to where I was staying and she got into her chauffeured car and left. To make matters worse, when

I got back to the B&B, my luggage was packed. It was sitting in the foyer with my bill already settled and paid for by ELC (Elliott Corporation). I told the host I was not planning to leave right now, and he said that my stay here was done.

I was devastated! Angrily I left and went to the airport and headed back to England. Not really understanding what happened and why would she turn cold towards me after reuniting all these years. Something was not adding up! Did the blood work come back negative? I needed to get to the bottom of this.

It is amazing how the woman that had taken me as an infant showed more love than my own flesh and blood.

With that thought in mind, I called home to speak with Cathy and check on mother. To my surprise, there was no answer. I called Cathy's cell phone and no answer as well. This was the longest flight ever to get back home. Perhaps I persecuted the wrong woman; perhaps I too was being rather selfish, consumed by my own thoughts and perseverance. I pray it will not be too late to apologize for abandoning her on her deathbed.

I just stared out the window looking into the clouds with watered filled eyes. Oh my God, what have I done?

Chapter Three

(At Home)

"Was all in vain?" Was what I was thinking. I had traveled a great distance to the United States, just to be let down again. As I approached my home, I felt this eerie chill come over me and I was praying my mother was still alive. I drove so fast I almost hit and oncoming vehicle. Seemed like, the more I drove, the longer the road. Finally I made it home and ran to the door to open it. Cathy was standing at the top of the stairs looking down at me. The countenance of her face was sad and she said,

"Your too late Alex, she's gone!"

My bags dropped to the floor, and it felt as if my heart dropped to my stomach. I ran upstairs to Cathy; she barely hugged me and turned her head from me when I kissed her cheek. Then she said, "Your mother died an hour ago, but not without leaving you some last words. She needed you! I needed you and you abandoned both of us". She handed me a letter, which I placed in my coat pocket. Her body was still in the bed with a physician writing a report and he even looked at me with disgust on his face. Dr. Winston was our family physician and knew us well. I walked over to my mother, held her, and cried, "I'm sorry" I must have said it a hundred times, before the coroner got there to pick up her body.

Cathy was in the kitchen on the phone talking to her twin brother Carlton before she started cleaning up and preparing for visitors. I walked in there, and she would not look at me. She was so angry and rightfully so; I did in fact abandon both women. Finally, I could not take to the silent treatment from Cathy and I begged her to talk to me. She became the voice of my mother and said

"Why should I Alex? Why should I show you more gratitude or mercy than you've shown your mother? Regardless of her trespasses she loved you—I love you, and yes Alex, she may have made mistakes but you did not let her explain. Maybe there was a reason she took you. But you never gave her a chance to explain. You thought only of yourself Alex, and finding Clarice. I hope this letter she wrote you will give you some peace and closure. But as for me, why should I show you more than you showed her? She loved you and I loved you, but we just were not good enough". "Cathy, I realize now that I was wrong. But you have to put yourself in my shoes. I have been deceived my entire life. When I discovered what she had done, I sort of snapped. Rage took over and yes, I wanted her to suffer. I never meant for this burden to land at your feet. I should have been here and I am sorry I wasn't" She slapped me. She told me "keep your sorry Alex" then she walked off and left with the doctor. I then called the funeral parlor to make the necessary arrangements for my mother. Nevertheless, Cathy had contacted them, and took care of everything as my mother had requested. She was to be buried the next day, next to her husband. I was lost and did not know what to do. Cathy came back over that afternoon and brought food. She had been cooking all morning making hors d'oeuvres for the reception at the house. Neighbors came by bringing food and Cathy was so gracious acting as the host. I, however, was feeling sorry for myself, ashamed and just standing around lost as ever. I have now successfully hurt two women who loved me unconditionally.

My mother has a gazebo in her back yard, and there is where I went to find solitude. I had her letter with me and I knew this was going to be difficult to read, but I had to. Cathy was watching me from the dining room window. I hesitated for a moment before reading the letter and to hear my mother's last words to me. I did not know if they would be words of anger, hurt, or a confession of some sort. Whatever it was, it was time for me to hear what she had to say.

My dearest son Alex,

If you are reading this letter, than I have failed as a mother. I have tried to shield you from the ugly truth for years of who you are and my role as a parent with you. As you know now, you are not my biological son, but I loved you nonetheless. I loved you the day you were saved in my arms from a horrible accident.

On so many occasions I wanted you to know the truth and I even wanted to give you back when you were a baby, but my selfishness would not permit it. For this I ask for your forgiveness and pray that God has forgiven me too. Today I am having a good day. I guess the morphine has numb all of my pain, allowing me to write this last epistle to you.

As you know, I was once married to a wonderful man name Alexander Bowles. Shortly after our marriage he left for war, leaving me with child. I prayed for him daily and our unborn child. God showed me in a dream everything would be okay and I would bear a son. Well, as I entered into my six month of pregnancy he was killed. Then to make matters worse, I miscarried and lost my baby. I didn't blame God at all. I knew *he would keep his promise and grant me a child—A son . . . A good son to be exact.*

Then a few months later, while driving home one night from work. I saw a bad car crash and explosion. Everyone looked dead. I was the first person at the scene and was horrified by this. I got out of the car and looked around. I heard an infant crying in the bushes some distance away. It was a beautiful baby boy, with little scratches on him. You looked at me like I was your savior. You were such a good baby and I took you home with me. You see, I thought this was the prophecy in my dream. We bonded instantly Alex. It wasn't until sometime had past that I heard about the survivors. By then it was too late. You were mine to behold.

One day when you were a little boy Clarice Elliott was here in England. It was the grand opening of the Elliott school and I wanted to take you there to reunite with her then. Before I could set off, you became very ill with the chicken pox. I took that as another sign from God that you were meant to stay with me.

I am sorry for all this, I am sorry for not telling you the truth and I hope one day you will forgive me even in death. Love mother.

After reading the letter, I cried thinking how insensitive I was to her, and how much she truly loved me. As wrong as she was to do what she did, I actually found myself sympathizing with her. My hurt turned into anger and I was plagued by the recent meeting with Clarice.

Cathy came outside, sat beside me in the gazebo, and asked if I were okay. I just laid my head on her shoulders and held her in my arms. Then I kissed her lips, got up, said, "I can't do this", And walked away. We were both in pain and it would have been very easy to make love to her, but I didn't want it this way. As I was walking away she yelled, "Why do you keep running away?"

I did not answer her, I just kept walking. The guests have left and Cathy had put everything away. Now I was all alone in this quiet and lonely home. I poured myself some brandy and sat in front of the fireplace. I sat there staring into the blazing fire until the last bit of flame burned out. Finally, I went upstairs and I placed the letter on my bedroom dresser and went to take a drive. Just before I left, I heard some noise down stairs and went to check into this. Cathy had come back to my home to return my sweater I left in the gazebo. She went into my bedroom to put away my sweater in the dresser drawer, and she saw the letter written from my mother. Cathy read the letter and realized she had to intervene so I can have some peace.

Cathy and I are very close, and as I looked upon her as a sister, she looked at me as a lover. I did not realize how much Cathy loved me, or just what lengths she would go through just to make sure I had peace.

Cathy wrote down as much information about Clarice Elliott that she could possibly find. At first she stayed up late looking up her genealogy on the computer. When I got back from my drive I saw she was using her laptop doing research in the guest bedroom, where she had been staying the last few days before my mother's passing.

That night she told me she would be leaving, but I told her she could stay here as long as she liked. Cathy told me "Alex, I have some family business to attend to and had to leave tomorrow".

"Is there anything I can do to assist? After all you were here for my mother and me. Let me return the favor".

"No, what I need to do, I must do on my own"

I nodded my head and I kissed her goodnight and retired to my room.

The next morning before leaving on her trip, we had breakfast together. She asked "How are things between you and your biological mother? Was everything resolved? Did she accept you back with open arms?" I told her "Everything started off well, but I did not like how we parted and I felt she did not want me around for financial reasons". "Perhaps, she felt you were out for her family fortune".

"You ought to see how lavish they are living. Maybe, I posed a threat to their lifestyle and I wonder if my father had left anything to me". "You would think that he would have left something to his son. Well Alex, I have stayed long enough and I have to go now". "Cathy wait! Please tell me where you are going? There is something I do want to talk to you about—Something I want to ask you"

"Well Alex, you're just going to have to wait until I return . . . Take care Alex"

I could see Cathy was very hurt about the situation and grew tired of me not being there for her, as well as not being there for my mother. I grabbed her coat, put it on her shoulder, and hugged her. She looked into my eyes and put her hand on my face as if she wanted to tell me something, but instead the tears in her eyes spoke volumes—Then she left.

I went into my mother's study and found her last will and testament. It was hard for me to accept what had happened and I could not bring myself to open it. So I just put the envelope in my coat pocket and took the will to her lawyer's office. The will stated that she was leaving me everything—the real estate and bank accounts, which totaled more than $365,000.00 pounds—And she left her jewelry to Cathy, which she gave to her while she was still alive. Her jewelry alone totaled more than $60,000.00 pounds which made me happy, because Cathy had well deserved it.

Meanwhile, Cathy had driven to the library to research Clarice Elliott and even drove to the old mansion. Cathy was relentless about getting information on people, a real Nancy Drew she was. When she and I were younger along with her twin brother, we use to pretend we were a couple of detectives and love solving mysteries and even as adults we would watch old programs about unsolved mysteries. But this would be one mystery that would prove to be fatal. She found a site on the computer, which was linked to Clarice. This site had some information about Clarice's history and those she was previously married to. She started to dig deep into her history and found the names of each husband. She was amazed to find out she had been married four times and all of her husbands were deceased. She knew she was dealing with an evil, wicked woman, a real black widow. She needed to get as much proof for me to prevent me from pursuing her again. The next day Cathy drove to the old mansion to see what she could discover about her. After all, women are more intuitive and better at snooping than men.

She waited until the coast was clear and the school was closed before breaking into the old decrepit mansion. She marveled at the items in there and the filth was overwhelming but she still kept snooping. Finally she entered the children's room, one for a girl and a boy's nursery. From the nursery window she could see an old large tree with two graves beside it. However, the window was dusty and dirty. She took the sleeve of her sweater and rubbed the window in a circular motion to get a better view. Then that is when an image appeared of a woman—Clarice standing there, right over her left shoulder behind her. She was dressed in black looking at Cathy quite evil with a tight lip smirk. She was speechless and frightened to death. Not being able to speak at that moment, Clarice said,

"Well child, look like you've just seen a ghost"

Then she said, "Do you believe in ghost's Cathy? This old mansion is very haunted". Cathy tried to walk past her but Clarice was no ghost, she grabbed her, and threw her back into the wall.

"Please forgive me for trespassing; I had no right to enter your home"

"Why are you in my home Cathy? I could have your head for entering this home uninvited," Extremely frightened, Cathy replied "How do you know my name?" "Because I know everything, except for why you're in my home" "I could leave and I will not tell anyone you or I was here".

"I wouldn't dream of it honey, but I do want to know why are you investigating me"

"I was curious about who you were and your relationship with Alex". Clarice asked "Did Alex, put you up to this? "NO! He does not even know I am here. In fact, how did you know I was here? I thought you lived in New York"

Clarice smirked at me and said "the computer site is one I created for nosey people like you. I brought you here Cathy. You are here because I wanted you here."

Clarice looked away for a second and then replied, "Stay awhile and have some tea with me" then all of a sudden I heard a teapot whistle going off. She said, "I'm not a vicious person Cathy, I just like to be left alone and do not like people prying into my affairs"

She opened the kitchen door, so I could walk in before her. Then Clarice walked to the kitchen and poured a small cup of tea for both of us. Her back was turned to me and I could not see what she was doing. I told her "I have to leave" and she politely said "Stay awhile Cathy and chat with me; after all you came here for me right? Well now you have me all to yourself". Also she said she would answer any questions that I had. So I looked at the door and thought maybe I could make a dash for it, but was too frightened to attempt. She poured herself some tea and sat down. My eagerness to get to the bottom of everything took over and I began to sip the tea and talk with Clarice. She then crossed her long legs and said, "What would you like to know about me?"

"Why did you deny Alex? He loves you and wants to start a mother-son relationship with you, why were you cruel to him in New York? He said that you were kind and then became cold towards him."

Before she could answer my questions, my vision became blurred, I felt extremely dizzy and started to feel faint. She asked me "how was my tea?" I could not answer her questions, because my mouth became numb and I could not speak. When I stood up and tried to walk I grabbed my chair and fell over onto the floor. My brain was trying to tell my body what to do, but my body could not respond. My limbs were too weak and numb as if I was dying, but my eyes were opened the entire time. The only thing that was working on me was my hearing. I could hear everything being said, but could not open my mouth or move my fingers. I realized I had been poisoned.

Just then Clarice had cleaned the two cups and poured the water out of the kettle. While I was lying lifeless on the floor, she was humming this tune very low and made a phone call. Moments later the door opened and a sheriff walked in. I felt I would be saved until he asked Clarice "Another one?" and she looked at him with her arms folded and said yes. She told him "Nancy Drew here was prying into my personal affairs—literally."

Then the sheriff said "Let me guess, a friend of Alex?" Then she nodded her head and said, "I believe it is his girlfriend. I do not know if I should end her life here or make her suffer". Just listening to them made me terrified; I could hear every word that was being said about me. I knew my life was at an end, she was going to kill me, probably like she killed her husbands. I just prayed and hoped Alex would come and save me.

As Clarice leaned over me; I could feel her cold breath in my face, as she said to me "You are going to die slowly after suffering first."

She told the sheriff I have a perfect place to store her, in my cellar so she can rot slowly. The sheriff picked up my lifeless body, and followed Clarice into the wine cellar. The wine cellar was below the mansion in a dark, cold and dreary room. Once they entered the cellar, there was another door hidden behind the wall wine rack. It was a secret room that was never completed. This door was made of old English wood and was impossible to break or even escape. The sheriff asked "What type of room is this?" "My husband built it; it was supposed to be a bomb shelter. But I made it into a storage room". When they entered the room, it was equipped with a toilet, sink, and a cot for sleeping. The sheriff laughed and said to Clarice "This is a perfect prison for this young lady here" "I suppose it will hold her for now. There is enough canned food to last for a year. Also, there is running water." The sheriff then laid me down on the cot and then they both walked out with Clarice locking the door behind them. The wall size wine rack went in front of the door to hide it. All I could think to myself was where was Alex?

Meanwhile, I was at home worried about where Cathy was. I called her brother Carlton and he had not heard from her as well. We both tried calling, texting and even emailing her—but there was no response. After a week had passed, Carlton came to see me. He wanted to know if we had a fight or did she go to visit Clarice. I responded to him no to all of the above. Cathy had no reason to visit my mother. Personally, I felt she was overwhelmed about my situation and losing my mother. Carlton was getting irritated that Cathy was so involved and consumed with my life, that she just left everything behind. This was so unlike her to be gone without notice. And not letting us know she was at least okay. We gave her one more week and still no word from her. Carlton and I went to the sheriff department and put in a missing person. We also drove out to the House of Elliott to see if anyone had seen her there.

I could not believe this was happening. I wept as I started to feel like I lost another true love in my life. I feared the worse that my Cathy was gone forever—Dead! That has been the story of my life with the women I have been close to. The complexities of all these situations were starting to take its toll on me and I was starting to lose it.

I felt my life was coming apart and there were no answers. Carlton was very distrusting and did not like the fact that I was close to his sister. He felt she was too good for me and wanted her to continue with school and live with him in Oxford. I could tell he was blaming me for his sister and really, who could blame him.

Poor Cathy, when she woke up from the toxic tea, she was all alone in a dark, cold, dreary, and isolated dungeon. She was too weak to scream and frightened that Clarice or the sheriff would return to finish her off. As time passed, she realized no one was coming to save her.

Chapter Four

(Redemption)

Carlton was heartbroken knowing his sister could be out there somewhere roaming. Was she in a hospital? Did something horrible happen to her? On the other hand, had she had enough of me and decided to go away and never be heard of again. All these questions were running through both of our minds.

Three weeks later, we went back to visit the sheriff in both counties. The sheriff in our county was very concerned about Cathy being missing and did everything he could to help. But when we went to see the other sheriff near the House of Elliott, he was less compassionate about her being missing. His lack of concern made Carlton and I very angry. Once we left the sheriff's department, Carlton and I went to the local diner. I could tell he wanted to ask me something so I said, "Carlton, what's on your mind?" he just reared back in his seat stirring his coffee and asked, "Did you kill my sister?" Stunned and outraged by that question, I frowned at him and said, "Carlton, I love Cathy and she loves me. I would never do anything to harm or cause harm to her. How dare you ask me that? I wanted to marry her"

"Because Alex, my sister was with you and stayed by your mother's side. Now all of a sudden—she's missing! You were the last person to see her alive."

"Carlton, I understand how it could seem that way, but I love her and would never do such a thing. You must believe me."

We both sat there in the café quiet from that point on, just eating our food. Torn by my emotions, I felt responsible for Cathy, but I would never reveal that to her brother. It was going on four weeks and no one has heard from her still. Now that a whole month has passed, I went to see the sheriff again. He asked me to sit down then he leaned back in his chair and said "how may I help you—Alex?" I asked him "Has there been any word on my best friend Cathy St. Claire? We still have not heard from her". He exhaled and said "Look son, we had our search team out looking for her in several jurisdictions. No one has heard nor seen Cathy. At this point we could only think that she maybe deceased" "NO, I shouted. I don't accept that! You are the same people that thought I was deceased years ago, and here I am!"

Then he asked me "Are you staying here in town?"

"Yes! I am going to be here as long as possible until I get to the bottom of Cathy's disappearance". The sheriff turned around and said, "I'm sorry about your friend. We searched everywhere for her, we even drove up to the mountains when I ran across a young lady lying down along the side of the road severely injured from a car accident. But it was not Cathy."

The sheriff said "look, as you can see the weather is bad and is getting worse. Nonetheless, we will continue our search for another week". He scratched his head, leaned forward towards me, and said, "If you think she was here, which I do not believe, her car would still be here. There have been an APB on her vehicle and I will notify you and Carlton once it or she is found".

"And Alex, don't go trespassing on private property" "Oh, you mean the House of Elliott?" "I think you know what I mean"

I sat back down and said, "Tell me sheriff, why are you so involved in that old rickety mansion?" The sheriff stood up angrily and said, "Look! It is my responsibility to protect the citizens in my jurisdiction. I am going to help you find your missing friend. However, that old house or any house in my town is OFF LIMITS! The next time I catch one of you outsiders snooping around that old house I'm going to throw your ass in jail".

I smirked and looked down at the floor shaking my head in disbelief. Then I said, "Catch one of you outsiders?—Well sheriff, I would like to know who has been out there to the house—Cathy?"

He became angry, and told me I needed to leave so he can continue his investigation. I hung around the town for about a week, and that is when I got a call from the sheriff's department. He told me that they have located Cathy's vehicle. Carlton received a call also and we both met at the department. When we arrived the sheriff showed us both pictures of her car—A 2006 red Volvo! Then he took us to the Airport where they were checking for fingerprints and doing there crime scene investigation. The car was parked in an area where there was no surveillance camera. Carlton rubbed his hair back and said to me "She left! All this crap you put her through made my twin sister up and leave." The sheriff said, "We checked various airlines for her name and there were no names registered under hers, I believe she may have used an alias and fled." I looked away and thought she could be anywhere, what have I done? Carlton was furious and said "I blame you for this Alex".

We both left and went back to the sheriff's department and asked him what was next? He replied, "Cathy is a grown adult. If this was a child then the circumstances would be different. But it clearly look like she left on her own accord" Deep down in my heart I felt there was more to this situation than he was leading on, but I could not be certain. Carlton did not trust me, and totally blamed me for this. I thought about going back to the House of Elliott, but it was well guarded and hard to get in.

The house was now under the protection of the sheriff's department and there was a deputy sitting outside guarding the premises. Then he called Clarice and explained the situation to her. He told her Carlton and I was suspicious and relentless about finding Cathy. And how he had taken her car to the Airport to give the illusion she had taken off. She told the sheriff that she trusted that he would take care of the situation and leave her name out of it. She also reminded him this was now his problem and not hers, and to keep us or anyone else out of her house. She had no problem reminding sheriff Cardone, that he owed her this.

Many years ago when the sheriff first started his job, he was patrolling the roads, and had fallen asleep while driving. He caused an accident by forcing one vehicle into another and then abandoned the scene. Clarice and Frances were the victims of that accident. The sheriff was so horrified that he caused such an accident that he felt obligated to her. Clarice was not sure who caused the accident because she was so overwhelmed with finding her child and saving the lives of her other two children. Years later the sheriff being overwhelmed with guilt confessed to Clarice and told her about his part of that horrible night.

Later that night, I went back to the house because I needed to make sure Cathy was not there hurt or imprisoned. I had a hunch that Cathy maybe there and I needed Carlton assistance to distract the sheriff in that jurisdiction. So while Carlton went to see the sheriff again to wrap things up. I had managed to give the deputy the slip when he fell asleep in his patrol car. I entered the house from the back through the window.

I searched profusely through items in the kitchen, bathroom, and bedrooms and found nothing. I even checked the cellar and saw nothing but a huge wall size rack of wine. I searched the upstairs liberally and did not see any sign of foul play. After my intense search of the house, I went back into the kitchen and sat down at the table to think what could have happened here and why are they protecting this property so much? Then, while sitting at the table I noticed something glittering on the floor. It was one of Cathy's earrings. I took the earring and put it in my pocket. I realized now without a doubt that Cathy was here and now I need to talk to my mother.

The earring was actually placed on the floor by Clarice to toy with me. She knew I would return to the house and I believe she wanted me to know; she had something to do with Cathy's disappearance.

I went back to my hotel room and waited for Carlton to return. Once Carlton returned, I showed him the earring and told him what I suspected. I said, "Carlton, I suspect Clarice was at the house and did something to Cathy—So tomorrow, I'm flying out to New York alone to confront her about Cathy's disappearance."

"If you are going, then I'm going with you."

"Carlton, things may get too dangerous and I do not want to involve you any further."

"I'm already involved! She is my blood and to think she might be dead behind you or this new mother of yours just sickens me that much more."

At this point I wanted him to return home. But Carlton was not going to adhere to that because that is his sister and he was not going to sit idle about the situation.

Before heading to New York to talk to Clarice, that same day I met with an attorney to find out what my legal rights were since I was the only son of Frances II. Also, I spoke with a criminal attorney regarding Cathy's mysterious disappearance since the sheriff's department was of no help. After being counseled by both attorneys', I knew I might be faced with the grim decision of pressing charges against Clarice, with little evidence. Just the thought of that made me feel quite ill.

The next day Carlton and I booked a flight to New York. I wanted to confirm that Clarice was in town the week of Cathy's disappearance. Also, I wanted to personally question her to see if I could catch her in a lie.

When we arrived in New York we checked into a hotel near Niece's department store. We waited for the opportunity to go inside, a time when it did not seem so busy. The receptionist notified Clarice that I was in the lobby. Instead of Clarice coming out to greet me, it was Laverne, but she was less than friendly this time. She at first welcomed me with a cold hug and then asked me if I made an appointment to see our mother.

She explained to me that mother is a very busy woman and one just cannot walk in at any time to see her. So, I asked "Lavern is mother by chance available right now?"

"Let me see Frances if she wants to see you. She's been very busy in and out of meetings all morning."

"Please let her know it is imperative that I speak with her"

After calling our dear sweet mother on her mobile, Clarice responded "Darling, I have a few minutes to spare so send him up". Carlton looked at me as if he could not believe this was my mother being so cold and distant. I then turned to Carlton and said, "I need to do this alone" and asked him to have a seat, so Carlton waited downstairs, and browsed around looking at some men's wear.

When I went upstairs to Clarice's office, she opened the door and said, "Frances, I am very busy. I wasn't expecting to see you so soon. What can I do for you?" "Well mother, you can start by telling me the truth" Then, I walked up to her and held my hand out to show her what was in it. She looked down at my hand and I slowly opened it, to reveal what was in my palm—It was Cathy's earring.

Clarice being quick witted and arrogant said, "Charming earring, but when people usually give me a gift, it's normally in a box and also it would have its pair!

And please tell me you didn't come this far to show me this earring?" I closed my hand quick and said

"You know who earring this belongs to and you have some explaining to do. I want you to tell me the truth about what happened to Cathy"

"Frances, how would I know what happened to Cathy? And, how am I supposed to know whom that ridiculous earring belongs to? I doubt seriously you purchased it in this building". I became angry after hearing her insults about Cathy's jewelry. Then said "This earring belonged to Cathy and do you know where I found it?" She shrugged and said "let me guess? On her ear! Then you would have two earrings right? Or does she have just one ear?" Not finding her comments amusing at all, I said "I found it at our family home. The House of Elliott—And, she's been missing for weeks now."

Clarice was not much surprised about where I found it, as much as she was surprised to hear me refer to the House of Elliott as *our home*. That was my way to annoy her back, which was very effective. Her eyes got big, dark and set back when I said our home. Keeping her composure she asked me "Why are you here Frances?"

"Because I believe you had something to do with her disappearance or know something about it, the local sheriff in that town is hiding something and you both are in on it".

Clarice said "How dare you! You came all this way to accuse me of your friend's disappearance? And if she was in my house, why was she there? And when did all this nonsense transpire?"

I told her the day everything had taken place and she laughed and said, "Look, I was here at work and left early because I became ill, it's all right here on my calendar—As for her trespassing the sheriff there should have shot her on the spot for breaking and entering. What was she doing in MY house?"

"She was trying to help me."

"Trying to help you, in my house? Look I am sorry about your mother and friend, but this is all a waste of my precious time. I am going to have to ask you to leave."

"Wait! There is one more thing mother. I found this earring in the kitchen of the house. The sheriff is of no help to me and he becomes very irritated when I question him."

"Well, there you go Frances; it sounds like the problem is with the sheriff. Had it ever occurred to you that the sheriff took her there or caught her there and tried to have his way with her? It sounds like sheriff Cardone is the one that should be questioned, not me".

I walked to her skyscraper window looking out and thinking, that would make sense that it could be the sheriff alone. Clarice kept her head down; as she knew the window would cast her image, of having a devious expression.

Then I turned around and said, "We also need to discuss another matter mother" she looked at me and felt this would be about money. So she said, "Make it quick, I have a meeting to attend"

"Okay, it is my share of the family fortune, E.L.C. Corporation which includes—The House of Elliott and Niece's!"

She sat down, reared back in her chair, and asked me "have you seen an attorney yet? And why do you feel entitled to anything I have?"

"Because, I am my father's only son and would have benefited from his death as you clearly have."

She was boiling on the inside and if there was a manifestation of something evil in her, it took everything for it not to come out and snatch my head off. She resorted to her tight lip smile and walked over to me and stood directly in my face and placed her hands on my shoulder and said "Alex, I don't know what happened to you, maybe the death of your mother or the loss of your friend has made you crazy. As for your inheritance, there is none. All this was built by my daughters and me and trust me when I say; you would not want Tranice to get wind of your accusations and threats about inheritance! Now get the hell out of my office!"

She opened the door and called security so Carlton and I could be escorted out onto the streets. Carlton looked at me and said, "It did not go well huh?"

"No, it actually went very well. I think the sheriff maybe the one responsible but; Clarice is not innocent in this matter either".

Meanwhile, Clarice called a meeting with her daughters to inform them of their brothers' accusations and to explain to them that she needs to protect their assets. Tranice said, "I knew it! It is always about money. This is why I wanted you to turn him away at the beginning, but instead, you welcomed him with open arms. He's an opportunist mother! I knew eventually he would show his true colors. But he will not get a dime of Niece's and Tony will make sure of that!"

"Good, make sure you have Tony to stay on top of that. I personally have some other matters to take care of. Cancel my meetings girls, I'm taking a vacation" Clarice left in her private jet and flew back to Europe to meet with the sheriff.

Tony Luciano is Tranice's husband, a very powerful and influential man. As a member of IMF (Italian Mafia Family), he had ways of dealing with people who posed a threat to him or his loved ones. Tony would not hesitate to make calls to assist his mother in law. On a few occasions, Clarice has had to call Tony for help.

When Clarice arrived in town she called the sheriff from a local phone and told him she needed to see him immediately. She knew now she had to frame him for Cathy's disappearance, because the police would be onto her and I was on her tail. She could use her charm and sex appeal on him. Once the sheriff got there she told him to come inside the House. He could see she was upset about something and began to tear up. They both walked into the kitchen and Clarice told him she felt scared that

Carlton and I were on to them and did not know what to do. He asked her "did something happen in New York?" She told him about the allegations that were made about her and his involvement in Cathy's disappearance. The sheriff became frustrated and said he was going to have to deal with me. Clarice not wanting to be involved in another murder began to cry, which was all an act of hers. The sheriff walked over to her and put his arms around her to console her.

She put her arms around his neck and started kissing him and things started to heat up. She would use her one weapon to seduce him. She then began to unzip his pants, as he was surprised by this outburst of affection and passion she was showing him. He started kissing her in return. While kissing him, she massaged his crotch until he had an orgasm in her hand. When he got through and went to the bathroom, she smeared what was left on her hands onto the floor precisely where Cathy's earring was found. Then, she walked over to the sink and washed the evidence off her hand.

Afterwards, he took pity on Clarice and promised her everything would be okay. He said he will have all the rooms cleaned and she said do not touch the kitchen because she will take care of that room. The sheriff agreed and she offered him some tea. She handed him a cup of her special tea which was drugged and she sat down at the table drinking hers watching him drink his. The sheriff had no idea he had just stepped into her web of deception. Drugging people has always been her first line of defense, to get the upper hand on people. As soon as the sheriff left and went back to his office, he called a cleaning crew to go to the House of Elliott and clean all the rooms except the kitchen. Clarice was making sure everything was in order there at the mansion to frame the sheriff. She made sure the cellar was secured as well as the door behind the wall of wine. Then she followed the sheriff to the police station and parked nearby to watch him leave for home. The sheriff had planned to catch up on some work. Suddenly he became very sleepy; he couldn't understand this sudden urge to sleep. He decided to go home to rest and come back later in the day. Clarice knew that the drug she put in his tea should have kicked in by now. The sheriff only lived 5 miles from the police station, but he couldn't keep his eyes open. He did not realize that he had been drugged. The sheriff started to fall asleep behind the wheel just before getting to his exit. He drove off the road and into the embankment and hit a huge tree. The impact of his head hitting the steering wheel was not fatal enough to kill him. But he was unconscious due to the concussion he had suffered. She walked up to him, grabbed his head from the driver's door, and slammed it again against the steering wheel causing him to die.

She left the scene and drove to the sheriff's home and put some items that belonged to Cathy in his home. Then, she drove back to the private airport and headed back to New York. Meanwhile, Carlton and I were heading back home to Europe. Once arriving home, I went to see the sheriff again and was told about the accident. Another officer investigating told me he wanted to talk to me about the case with Cathy. The investigating officer told me that not only was the sheriff dead from a fatal car accident, but he felt the sheriff was the cause of Cathy's disappearance.

Meanwhile, Clarice was sitting comfortably on her jet sipping her tea and thinking how much these situations can prove to be stressful. She called her girls, Lavern and Tranice, and assured them all was well in Europe.

Carlton and I stayed there in town until this was resolved. I could not believe how quickly things were unfolding. I felt our presence and not giving up made the sheriff very uncomfortable and caused him to panic. Maybe Clarice had notified him about our visit to her. After a couple of days of investigating, it proved that the sheriff was not the man they thought he was. Then they found out he ordered the House of Elliott to be cleaned and he ordered a cleaning crew to go in before the forensic team could complete their investigation. The investigation found the sheriff's semen stains there on the kitchen floor and concluded he may have raped Cathy at that location. Also, even though there was no surveillance camera at the airport. A security guard came forth and said he remembered the sheriff driving Cathy's car and parked it. It was not looking good for the sheriff and they ruled the case of foul play with him. The Internal affairs investigator felt he caught Cathy there and she must have refused his sexual advances, and he raped and murdered her. They also felt that there might have been other women the crooked cop had done this to and that he was using that place to do his evil deeds. He told me that Cathy was at the wrong place at the wrong time. This was making Carlton sick and mentally broken; he did not want to pursue it any further. He felt his sister was in Heaven and that was good enough for him. Clarice framed the sheriff for her wrong doings to be cleared of all suspicion by me.

When I thought about everything, it made sense. Cathy had been drugged by the sheriff, and her earring being on the floor was a sign as if there were a struggle. How he was over protective about the house and not wanting us there. In my mind, Clarice was cleared from having anything to do with Cathy's demise. Her only part in this is that Cathy probably went there to talk with her about me. She loved me and always cared about my wellbeing . . . Even if it cost her-her life! That will haunt and trouble me forever.

Chapter Five

(Clarity)

When we were kids, Carlton, Cathy and I use to ride our bikes to this big old English Oak tree down the road from our house. This tree had to be more than a hundred years old. It was our own community tree house. We would climb the tree and stay up there for hours on end—talking and telling jokes with one another. I remember I once snuck a kiss from Cathy in that tree when she was about ten years old. That was the day Carlton fell from it and broke his leg and Cathy and I carried him home. It saddens Carlton and I that we did not have a body to give Cathy a decent burial. So, before Carlton left—I told him I was going to make a memorial place by the tree. Though he was very grief stricken, he thought the gesture was nice. Next to the huge oak tree, we planted all of Cathy's favorite flowers—daisy's, tulips, roses and gardenias. Then, we put a white iron bench in the midst of the flower garden with a brick passageway leading to it. Finally, on the huge oak tree I carved the words;

In memory of our beloved Cathy Diana St. Claire June 19, 1982-October 2012.

Once I was done with carving a memorial into the tree, I etched a heart around the wording. That gave me a since of closure and I know she would have loved it. Once we were done, Carlton began to cry. I tried my best to console him but he was overcome by hurt and anger that there was no body for his beloved twin. Then we sat out there for hours, reminiscing about all the times we had at this tree. I felt her spirit was here in this beautiful place we created for her. As for me, Cathy's death made me become very heart broken and depressed, being I have lost the two women who cared about me more than anyone. The next day Carlton went back home and tried to accept all that had happened but something was not right with him. He had a hard time dealing with the loss of his twin sister, and I know deep down he blamed me.

Days and weeks later I became a recluse and would have haunting nightmares about Cathy and my mother. I would constantly feel their presence in this lonely home of mine. Then I began having gut wrenching nightmares as if they were both trying to warn me about something.

The dreams were so realistic and haunting. I often had nightmares of being trapped in the House of Elliott, hearing Cathy's voice calling me. I knew that there was an evil presence there other than Clarice and it made me ill. Then there was this other dream where I was lying in bed, then all of a sudden red liquid turned my white sheets to blood red. And Cathy was standing at the foot of my bed, but it was not blood at all—I was drowning in red wine. What did all this mean and why was I having these types of dreams?

These nightmares were ongoing for days causing sleep deprivation. I would stay up at night and drink coffee just to avoid falling asleep. I had no peace and my appearance showed it. My hair had grown long again, I had a beard and I started losing weight rapidly. I had to see a therapist because my nightmares and depression was leading me in a downward spiral. The medications that the doctor had given me for sleeping were not working either. The therapist felt I should resolve issues with my mother. But I could not bring myself to go through that again with her and be rejected. At our last visit or confrontation, she made it quite clear that she did not want anything to do with me. However, the nightmares would not stop, and this went on for a couple of months. Finally I decided to follow my therapist advice, and try once more to see Clarice. I needed closure and to resolve matters with her once and for all, and move on with my life.

I needed to assure her that I was never after her money or material things. Having her acceptance would be nice, and giving me an opportunity to apologize for my accusations would be even better. Meanwhile back in New York, Clarice had spoken to an advisor regarding the property. She was told settling would be in her best interest because of the possible negative publicity. She did not like that advice at all, so she had to come up with a master plan that would be beneficial for both of us. Among everything that Clarice is, she is an opportunist who knows how to invest wisely. She knew the facts were that she had not heard from me for a few months. I believe she feared I would return one day, and this was far from over. Perhaps she thought someday she would be subpoena to court regarding a lawsuit or settlement; one thing was for sure, she did not want any more surprises from me.

While I was dealing with my depression, Clarice again was plotting how to save her house from me and what would be the best solution. After talking with her daughters, they decided to renovate the old mansion and turn it into a museum. Lavern felt there was such a charm about the place. In addition, it had the reputation of being haunted, which would attract people to it. Clarice brainstormed the idea and talked with her attorney about all the living interest in the property and her heirs. The attorney told her to add me to the property using my real name (Frances Elliott) and as for her will, that it didn't matter as long as she left me a small percentage, even as low as 1%. She felt as if I had the upper hand, and conspired with both daughters Tranice and Lavern to strategize a plan. This outraged Tranice and she told her mother to deal with this the way she knows best, but Clarice told her daughter that the killing stops here. She explained she barely got away with the last one being the sheriff, and is getting too old for this. Tranice told her "Mother, have Tony take care of Alex" but Clarice told her "no!" Lavern said, "Look mother, just leave him a small percentage. We are okay with that!" However, not Tranice she stormed out of the office, and threw her hands up and said, "Make sure you keep him away from me."

Then, Lavern asked her mother "why do you despise him so? After all, the blood test proved that he is your son. Could it be because he reminds you of yourself and you cannot stand it? I mean he is very persistent like you and he never gives up."

"Are you deliberately trying to annoy me this morning Lavern? Truth of the matter is, he reminds me of your father and it breaks my heart looking at him" then she began to cry. Clarice asked Lavern to leave her alone, while she thinks about what she is going to do. She then walked over to her mother and hugged her and said, "There is a simple remedy for this, you just need to realize it. Open your heart to him mother and stop resisting him, after all he is your son. Try to work things out with him; you know father would want it that way."

"You are right Lavern; I have been such a fool. I need to make things right again. Perhaps, I should take some time off work and go visit him."

Later that day she told her daughters she was going to take a vacation and go to Europe, so she could have some clarity and make things right again. During her long flight, she thought about Cathy being locked away in her cellar. She stayed in the old house for a week cleaning up all the mess, spider webs and getting rid of old furniture and bringing in new items. Then, she sat at the table sipping her tea and thought about how life was supposed to have been from the beginning. She took it upon herself to finish what her beloved husband had started which was a bed and breakfast. She opened all the windows to let light in where darkness once was. She just stared out of the window thinking, "What should I do with Cathy? How long should I keep her locked away?"

After a couple of weeks of being in seclusion, I decided to drive out to the house for no apparent reason. For some unknown reason, I was simply drawn to that house. Maybe it's because it was the last place Cathy was at. When I arrived, I saw that the house was repainted and the landscape outside was well manicured. The old white decrepit picket fence was torn down and replaced with a black iron fence, giving the house an elegant look. So, I drove up to the newly paved driveway and knocked on the door. To my surprise, Clarice answered the door. She stood there looking at me with a pleasant look on her face. Yet another shade of her personality!

"Hello mother"

"Frances, please come in, I'm happy to see you"

I smiled as she greeted me warmly, unlike our last meeting. I am drawn to this woman, I need her in my life and I don't know why. As I stood in the foyer and she took my jacket, I looked around and saw how beautiful and refreshed the place looked. Even the painting of her and my father was restored. It was in a new frame and well exposed in the living room area over the fireplace. I asked, "What happened here?" "I'm starting over son," she told me "I needed to come back and regroup. I needed some clarity and this place has always been special to me". Then she offered me some tea, which I gladly accepted. She asked me to sit down with her while she was preparing the tea for two. Her disposition was different today, even more so than the time when we met at our first dinner. She was kind and warm. This woman has so many shades about her. Almost like split personality—nonetheless, I want her in my life.

She handed me my tea and said, "Alex, I'm sorry for how I behaved before and the things I said. This whole situation happened to quickly for me. I resented you for the wrong reasons, maybe for not being Frances when you look so much like him. On the other hand, maybe because you were stolen by another woman and I really did not know how to deal with your love for her. I know you loved her, even after all she had done and she was the only mother you knew. I felt betrayed by both of you, however, it was not your fault and I feel you have paid enough in your lifetime. So, with that said, I want to make amends and make things right. Can we start all over? I need you as my beloved son, and I will be your beloved mother. I can fill that void in your heart—Please give me that chance".

She had stood up and walked over to the painting with her back facing me in shame and her head held down. I exhaled looking at her from the back and saw an honest person this time. I walked up behind her and put my arms around her waist and said, "Not only do I forgive you mother, I need you also, and thank you for accepting me back into your life—I can't live without you."

Like a moth to a flame, I was drawn to her. Just then she turned around with tears in her eyes and hugged me, which felt sincere and compassionate for the second time. It seemed as if tears of joy or relief ran down her face and she stood back and said "we have so much to talk about and so many things to make right. I have so many things to tell you about my life, and more importantly your father and who he was. He would be proud of you son". Then she took my hands and called me Frances III and smiled. Then she asked me "would you accept your rightful name? Alex does not suite you and frankly my dear—I hate it!"

I lifted her chin upward towards me and said "Yes, mother! I want to be your son Frances".

Clarice said "let's propose a toast to my son—Frances Elliott III" Then I watched her walk away to the kitchen as she was pouring a glass of champagne. I stared at the painting ahead and said, "My father and I were mirror image of each other, it is rather spooky".

"Yes, you are Frances, which was a problem for me when you returned. It was as if he came back from the grave. The girls are a spitting image of me and you are of your father"

As I took my glass of champagne and tilted it towards me I said, "Alexandria could never tell me anything about my supposed father except that he was killed in the military. It will be nice to hear more of your stories about my real father."

"I have an idea, why don't you stay here a few days so we can share our stories and get to know each other all over again. I have many rooms in my mansion son and you are welcome to enjoy all of them."

"That would be nice mother; after all, I do have many questions to ask you"

I did not have any change of clothes because I was drifting that day; I went into town and bought a few items. That first night we stayed up quite late talking about each other's lives. Clarice told me how she met my father. The type of man he was and who his family was. Then, she told me how he built this home with his bare hands. As she talked about him, I could see a glow in her eyes that was passionate and loving. No man could ever compete with him or take his place in her heart, though many have tried. I loved hearing the stories about my father and I realized how much I was like him. I liked to build, stubborn, analytical and I was smart in math like him.

It seemed like the missing pieces in my life were finally starting to fall into place. Then while we were talking, I asked Clarice a question;

"Mother Clarice, did you have anything to do with Cathy's death?" I had to ask again while she was in a good mood. I needed to know the truth and only she could tell me.

"Possibly, but not in the way you think. The sheriff was obsessed with me and even this house. The sheriff would do almost anything for me if he felt I was threatened. I used to give the sheriff a stipend for protecting this old manor for me. I mean he guarded it as if it was his so I thought. Who knew he was bringing women here to do whatever. I am still very disturbed about the things he did. I suppose when Cathy came here somehow she crossed a line with him and he did what he did. So to answer your question, did I have anything to do with her death? The honest answer would be, possibly, and I am sorry for that son. However, I do feel Cathy's spirit is still right here in this house with your father"

"Well, that is an honest answer and I will accept that and forgive you mother. But I miss her so much and had planned on marrying her and starting our own family". I noticed she started to feel uncomfortable and fidgety then said, "Well son, we have been up late and need to get some much needed rest. We'll resume in the morning—Good night!"

I walked upstairs to my room thinking about Cathy. Clarice on the other hand was feeling nauseated about Cathy and lying to me about her. The next morning when I awoke I smelled hot coffee brewing and blueberry muffins baking. It reminded me of Alexandria. I washed up and came downstairs for breakfast. Clarice was humming a cheerful tune and setting the table for us to have breakfast together. She had prepared scrambled eggs and homemade blueberry muffins. Then we both sat down to eat together. She said, "Son, I was thinking. I am going to give an intimate party in a couple of days with the family to introduce you to our family . . . The Elliott's" "I spoke to your sisters this morning and told them to be here with their daughters to welcome you officially into the family as their beloved brother. I hope that's okay with you?"

"Of course mother, whatever you wish."

"Good! And at that time, I have a surprise for you as well."

Being that we had gotten up early that morning, she made calls to the girls and granddaughters to be here for her party, which, they of course had accepted. "So mother, what is on the agenda today?" "Well, I am going to take you to have a makeover and shopping. If you are going to be an Elliott, you must look as an Elliott" and she kissed my cheek, and we left.

I had this concerned look on my face, like what just happened and what did I get myself into? My cute little mother is such a snob, but it was starting to grow on me and I liked it. She called her European hairstylist and made an appointment for both of us. Then we went shopping at the Niece's store here in Europe and other high fashioned tailor shops. We were a cute mother and son couple for that day, as she was cloning me to become the perfect Elliott.

Chapter Six

(Heir to the name)

Watching mother prepare for the dinner party, gave her a sense of pleasure that she had not felt in a long time. Deep in her heart she was relieved to know that the name Elliott would rightfully live on through me. Though the family is predominately all women, the name must be carried on by a male and she was happy to have her son back to continue the family name. The day of the dinner party, Clarice left out early that morning for a business meeting with a hotel designer and architect. She wanted to discuss the surprise she had waiting for me. My sisters Lavern and Tranice arrived, as well as other family members and guests from New York. The daughters were in great suspense to hear our mother's announcement. The servants and the chef for the day had arrived, and Clarice spared no expense for the menu. It was a combination of various foods such as French and Italian cuisine. She also spared no expense on the champagne—Dom for everyone. Cocktails were at 6:00pm and her guest started to arrive. When her servant opened the door Clarice and I were standing there to greet everyone. Mother was wearing a long beautiful black evening dress that was strapless, and I was in my tailored tuxedo.

The first to arrive was Lavern and Neicey; they could not take the suspense any longer and did not want any surprises in front of their guests. They wanted to have a chat with mother but she was too busy entertaining. Minutes later, more family members started to arrive, until the room was filled with Elliott's. I had no idea that my family was this large, between my sister's spouses, their children, and our extended family members—This was quite the reunion.

There was light classical music playing which complimented the candle lit room, and gave it a warm and cozy ambiance. Though mother was very happy, I felt a little uncomfortable around all these aristocratic people. I really did not know anyone other than my sisters and a niece I had seen once before—Shay. Mother had asked her granddaughter, Shay, to play a selection on the grand piano for the guest. She went on about how her precious granddaughter was a graduate of Julliard and played for the Queen once. The guests were quite impressed as Most of the guests took a tour of the house, which they had admired. The craftsmanship of the late Frances Elliott was highly esteemed, as the newly hired contractors were able to refurbish and duplicate most of the work he had done.

This was an event long overdue in Clarice's mind, something that should and was supposed to have happened when her husband was alive, 30 years ago. She only wished that he could have lived to see his dream come true. Now that everyone had mingled and had his or her share of bubbly, Clarice stood in the living room in front of an easel tapping her crystal glass. It sounded like a dainty chime with every tap of her spoon. After getting everyone's attention, she said "My dear guest, family, and friends, I have an announcement and toast I would like to make. First, for those who do not know, I have been recently reunited with my son. He was separated from me when he was a baby. Please welcome my son—Frances Elliott III"

Everyone clapped and was stunned by the level of resemblance of my late father. (Earlier that week, Clarice had the local community newspaper print an article about the reunion of her and me) I felt honored in addition to nervous; however, I was starting to enjoy the attention. Then she said, "Secondly, we are going to be expanding this mansion into a luxurious hotel". At that moment she removed the sheet off the easel and exposed what the design of the new House of Elliott would look like upon completion. It was a grand five star hotel, which will feature the old mansion as part of its museum. Everyone applauded Clarice, including her daughters for making their fathers dream a reality. Then, she looked at me and said "My dear son Frances, will you be head of this project and assistant chief chairperson for all the House of Elliott manors?" I humbly nodded my head yes and walked over to mother and gave her a kiss on the cheek accepting her offer. Then, she smiled back at me and asked me to stand with my two sisters Lavern and Tranice, then she told everyone "A toast to the Elliott family & The House of Elliott"

"Lavern looked at Tranice, who had a smirk on her face, and feeling somewhat skeptical about this whole situation. Lavern whispered to Tranice, "Do not let your horns show sister and please do not make any disparaging comments" she looked at Lavern and whispered to her "I will hold my comments for now"

Clarice said, "Let us all adjourn to dinner now". Everyone all adjourned to the formal dining room and was seated for dinner.

The dinner went well and the food was scrumptious, and then it was followed by dancing. I could tell Tranice was standoffish so I walked over to her and asked her to dance. She gladly accepted because she wanted to talk to me up close and personal, and I wanted to talk to her. She whispered in my ear "I guess this worked out for you after all Alex, I mean Frances!"

"Listen Tranice, I was never after our mother's money or wealth, but things just turned out this way. Is it so hard to believe and accept me as your brother? And you must know, all I ever wanted was her acceptance and love"

She just looked the other way then turned to me and said, "Look, I don't care what my mother does with her time or money. You just do not hurt her any more than what she has already been hurt or bring shame to our family. She has been through a lot in her lifetime and she will do anything to help or save her child. We are all she has and she expects us to live up to her expectations. It is not easy being an Elliott and you will soon learn that. You will have to sacrifice for our namesake as she has sacrificed for ours. Are you willing to do that Frances? Our world is very different from yours. There will be times when you even have to go against your own principals and morals. I mean really, even the woman you marry will have to meet her approval".

"What are you saying Tranice? I'm not at liberty to marry whom I choose?"

"Exactly Frances, you just cannot bring any one into our family. If mother doesn't think she is worthy, she will not stand for it. Which brings me to the next question, do you think you can live up to our expectations? If you cannot, you should walk away now and move on with your life. Well, I have said enough and don't mean to bring you down on such a festive occasion. But think about what I have said"

Then Tranice walked away and left me standing on the dance floor. She walked over to Lavern, and told her about our conversation. Lavern and Tranice were sipping their champagne looking back at me, with a devilish smirk on their face. Clarice saw what had happened and walked over to me and asked me to dance with her. While we were dancing she asked, "Are you okay? Your sister's aren't giving you a hard time are they? Please don't let Tranice damper your spirits. She really means well, you just have to get to know her. She will eventually come around son" I just held my mother and said "not at all, they're just being over protective sisters and protecting the family interest—you!"

Everyone was having a great time with the festivities, as the evening was getting late. As the evening was coming to an end and everyone was beginning to leave, mother and I stood at the door thanking everyone for coming and well wishes. As the butler was putting Tranice's mink coat on, she was facing me and said, "I hope you thought about what I said brother."

"I'm pondering over it right now, dear sister" Though I was thinking, what an evil bitch she is!

She smiled, then she kissed our mother and left. I was troubled about the marrying part of our conversation because everything else I could handle. The only person I ever thought about or could have married was Cathy. I would never betray or hurt my mother now, not after all we have gone through. While I was deep in thought looking out of the window, Clarice asked "Frances did you enjoy the evening?" "Yes mother, you really out did yourself, and everything was wonderful" "And how do you feel about the new upcoming hotel, which should open next fall?", "You took me by surprise. I have never managed a hotel before and I definitely was not expecting it, however I am very grateful for your generosity. I promise I will make you proud of me".

She was pleased with that answer and told me "I will have someone from our corporation E.L.C. to train you with the family business. But for now son, I am going to retire to my room" she kissed me on my cheek good night, as I watched her walk upstairs to her room. Later that night after having some brandy, I adjourn to my bedroom and sat at the edge of my bed, holding a picture of Cathy. I could not help but think of her, realizing how much she loved me and that I loved her and would have married her. Now, I feel finding true love in my present circumstance will be a difficult task. Never really knowing if the person loved me for whom I am or greed. Clarice stayed there for a couple of more days with me, met with her attorneys, and told me she cannot wait to see the final remodeling of the home. I now had access to funds I could not have imagined; however Clarice was a dual signature to the account for anything over $1,500,000. She had opened a special trust account with her and I as the trustees to do business, with her approval of course.

Before she had left, she told me "thank you for coming back into my life and forgiving me for all those mean things I had said". "It is all behind us and I love you. Now you have a safe trip back to the U.S." She left and I began overseeing one of the biggest projects of my life—

The New House of Elliott

In New York at Niece's Corporation, the two sisters were talking. Lavern had asked Tranice "what are your thoughts about mother's change of heart towards Frances and him overseeing the House of Elliott project?"

Tranice, with a smug, looked said "mother is not fooling anyone, that was all for show, however we do need a male sibling to bear the name Elliott, but I think it was all for show" Lavern looked at her sister and said "I think she is reliving her dreams through him because he is identical to father" "Lavern please! Mother only cares about herself then us. She knew all along she would bring him into our fold it was just a matter of time, but the question is why? It's more than bearing the name Elliott. Also, I can't believe she gave him access to a trust account, with a limit of $1.5, who does that?"

"Money is no object to mother Tranice—But do you think mother had anything to do with the recent death of Cathy?"

"Oh dear God! Another dreadful person! Who knows and who cares. Mother deals with situations the best way she see fit"

Tranice walked to her window looking at her skyline view, then tilted her head to the side and said, "Really Lavern, mother showed me a picture of her and she knew that Frances was madly in love with her, and mother did not want her in the family or in the gene pool of future

Elliott's. I believe that is why mother made sure she was out of the picture for good."

"Now watch mother find him a woman, someone that is gorgeous, smart, and Italian of course" Just then Clarice came into Tranice office where the girls were having their conversation about her. Clarice said "Girls! I was thinking we need to have a mixer with a group of models, so that I can choose a proper wife for Frances."

Lavern looked at Tranice and said, "You know mother all too well"

Tranice said, "Mother are you serious? I am much too busy to be looking for a wife for Frances. This is Lavern's department, not mine" Lavern then said, "Let me guess Italian, beautiful and smart mother?"

"That is right Lavern; I want the works before he finds someone himself. And no telling what he would pick. After all, this is the family genes we are talking about. And make sure she is tall, at least 5'9 Lavern"

Mother walked out of the office and I told Tranice "Well sister, I better put this on the high priority" then walked out. Tranice just shook her head in disgust and went back to reading her reports. I had received many pictures from all over the country for models, but I focused solely on the Italian and American Italian models only. I was looking for the very best for my brother. There were several that I thought were beautiful and read their profile to see who was most educated. After I found a few to my liking, I took the photos and profile to mother to review. Mother liked all except for one who favored Cathy and told me to proceed and to have a mixer for Frances. She told me "Call your brother and let him know I am hosting a private party".

Chapter Seven

(Choosing wisely)

After weeks into overseeing the hotel, mother called me and asked me to come to New York and visit her. She explained that she was giving a small gathering and wanted to introduce me to a few of her guests. Not wanting to disappoint her, I flew to New York to spend a few days with her and attend her private party. The private party was held at her penthouse where I was staying. Attending the party was Lavern and several other women that she had chosen for me to meet. Mother was very pleased with the turn out and how beautiful in person these girls were. She felt Lavern did an excellent job putting this mixer together. She introduced me as her eligible bachelor son and personally introduced me to each girl. I felt like I was there to judge a modeling contest and I was the prize. They were all very interested in me, but as I feared for what reason? Were these women looking for a career advancement or greed! Lavern sat back and watched the show as mother work the room like a Madame. As much as I tried to get into this soiree, my heart was with Cathy. Finally after talking to a few of the girls, I seem to have shown an attraction to the one that Lavern thought would be perfect for me. She was somewhat standoffish, while the other ladies were a bit more aggressive. Clarice was pleased with how the mixer was turning out and told me "Son, this evening was meant for you! You've been alone long enough and need to find yourself a love interest. I handpicked these women especially for you. So honey, choose wisely and enjoy yourself".

"Mother, I can't thank you enough, and you are right. It is time for me to move on"

I did just that, and enjoyed myself with Helena and we seemed to hit it off right off the bat. While the ladies were all socializing with each other I took Helena out on the terrace so we could talk more privately. I told her after tonight, I would like a see her tomorrow. She accepted. I took her to a quiet romantic French restaurant in the city called Le Chateau. Helena was from Naples Italy; and spends a great deal of her time in Europe modeling and attending school. She was beauty personified with a genteel demeanor about her. I told her "I have always wanted to visit Naples, but never had a chance, due to my mother's illness. And now, I've been so busy with our new hotel in Europe" "You said your mother's illness? I wasn't aware that Clarice was sick" "I'm sorry Helena, I didn't mean my mother Clarice, I meant the woman who raised me. But that's a long story and I will share that with you someday" She told me left Naples when she was eighteen to attend Oxford University. Straightaway, I thought about Cathy. That is where Carlton wanted his sister to attend school before her demise. Helena told me her major was literature and she wanted to become a teacher. But one day while shopping at Niece's was approached by their beauty consultant and was eventually offered a job. I enjoyed our conversations—she was beautiful, had a nurturing quality about her, which reminded me of Cathy. Maybe that is was why I was truly attracted to her. Over the next few weeks, we were inseparable. I thought I would never start to feel about another woman the way I felt about Cathy. One day, when she came to visit me, I took Helena for a walk at a nearby park. She asked me

"Have you ever been in love before?" I smirked and said, "Yes, with my childhood sweet heart. Her name was Cathy! She was beautiful, warm, caring and thoughtful—like you" "You said 'was'. Did something happen to her?" "Yes, she was murdered by a sheriff

"Oh my God, that is horrible"

"Yes it was, and her body was never found. She was very special to me and I never thought I would find love again, until I met you." "I'm sorry Frances about what happened to her. I know that had to be very difficult to deal with, being you loved her and all" then she took my hand and we continue to walk around the park.

Lavern told Tranice that the mixer was a success and I chose the girl that she liked the most. Nevertheless, Tranice as always was skeptical and hoping things would turn out for the best for mother's sake. She knew how much our mother depended on this and me moving forward with my life and having a family. Mother is very adamant about her children having their own family. Deep down she wants us to be happy and having the best life has to offer.

I had returned to Europe to work and made frequent visits to Italy to visit Helena. For the second time, I was falling in love. Mother was hoping to hear from me soon regarding a proposal. That is how mother is, she believes in moving quickly if it is something you truly want.

Weeks turned into months, and my relationship with Helena was growing stronger each day. We would spend hours on the phone talking with one another. And if we weren't on the phone, we would be emailing each other. Mother hired Helena as the permanent model and spokesperson for their new line of Italian fashion. Helena was grateful for the generosity that was shown to her. And in no time we had fallen in love with each other. As time progressed, the hotel was almost completed after a year of dedication and hard work. One night after a year of dating steadily, I prepared a romantic evening at the old mansion. It was a candle lit environment, with soft music playing and food preparing. When Helena arrived she looked stunning wearing a dark blue evening dress with a low cut back.

After pouring her a glass of champagne and listening to romantic music, I took her by the hand and walked out onto the terrace with her. As she was gazing into the starry night, I was gazing at her because she was simply that stunning. Then I got down on my knees, pulled out a small box, and asked Helena "Will you marry me?" Before she answered she took my hands, then she touched my face, said, "Yes, I will be your wife", and gently kissed me on my lips. That night was simply beautiful. She spent the night with me, and we made love. The next morning I called mother and Lavern and told them the exciting news that Helena and I were engaged and are going to be planning a wedding, once the hotel was completed. Helena and I wanted to have our reception in the new grand ballroom. Clarice flew out to the new site to see how things were coming along and was very pleased with the new renovations and addition to the House of Elliott. Mother comes to visit often, usually once a month. She often goes to the wine cellar to restock with her favorite wine. She told me once, that she finds solitude down there. I guess because it is the most secluded spot of the house. I always give Clarice her space, even though I do wonder, "What does she do in there?"

"Now it was time for marketing strategies" mother said to me. There was an announcement in the newspaper about the grand opening of The House of Elliott Hotel. Meanwhile, In Oxford, Carlton had read about the upcoming grand opening and could not believe what he was reading. The article was about my engagement and upcoming marriage. It all seemed so perfect for me with a happy ending, while his sister seem to be forgotten. This infuriated Carlton while his sister was gone, murdered. He felt this was so unfair especially knowing how she took care of my mother and how much she loved me. He could not handle my success and new life. One day feeling depressed, Carlton drove back to our old town where his sister's memorial was. As he went to the garden we prepared for her, he sat down in the midst and he vowed he would avenge her death; someone was going to pay—Clarice!

Later that evening Carlton went to dinner and while at the restaurant he ran into my fiancé and me. I was excited to see him and greeted him with a handshake and hug, but he seemed resentful towards me. He was quite cold, and barely wanted to shake my hand. I then introduced my fiancé to him and he looked at her evil and cold, which sent chills up her spine. He then slowly took her hand and kissed it. I thought he was going to bite her hand the way he looked at her.

Afterwards, I asked Carlton "would you like to join us for dinner?" and Carlton said, "No thank you Alex, I have something I needed to take care of. I only came to town to visit Cathy's memorial. It is our birthday!" "I'm sorry Carlton, I forgot today was her and your birthday"

"No problem Alex and congratulation on all of your success. I see life has treated you exceptionally well" then he walked off abruptly.

While sitting with my fiancé waiting for mother to join us. I kept feeling this uneasiness about Carlton walking off, thinking there was something very unsettling about his behavior and I was concerned. Helena asked me "Why did he call you Alex rather than Frances? Did he not know you've changed your name?" "Yes, I'm sure he knows. But I will always be Alex to him" "Hmmm Interesting" "Yes, he was rather interesting"

As Carlton was walking out of the restaurant Clarice was just arriving and noticed Carlton. Instead of going into the restaurant, she decided to follow him. She saw how angry and disgruntle he looked and she did not trust him. Her instincts proved to be right because he drove to the new hotel and was sitting there in his car drinking alcohol and staring at the old mansion. He was drinking whiskey and looking disgruntled. Clarice being appalled by this behavior and watched him carefully from a distance to see what he was going to do next, but instead he drove off. She then called me on my cell phone and said, "Son, I'm glad you answered. I'm not going to be able to join you for dinner tonight. I am feeling a little ill. I'll see you when you get home.

"Okay mother, is there anything I can do for you? Maybe I can order you some soup or something?" "No son, it's probably delayed jet lag or maybe even a little bug" "Take care mother and I will see you soon".

She was now concerned that Carlton was going to cause some kind of trouble either at the upcoming grand opening or at the wedding. She needed time to think about how she was going to deal with him, where it would not come back on her or me. When I came home after dinner, I mentioned to mother that I had ran into Carlton. I also told her he seemed to be angry about something when he left. She told me "Not to worry son, Carlton is probably still mourning his sister, and seeing you with another woman could have been difficult for him" "Perhaps you are right mother. But, I am concerned" Then she asked "Frances darling, do you intend on inviting him to the grand opening or your wedding?" she said with a frown "Definitely!"

She sighed and said, "Look son, I know you to were close friends, but I don't think it would be appropriate given the circumstances and all. He might not be able to handle it and cause a scene, and we wouldn't want any embarrassments on your special day"

"Perhaps, you're right. I'll think about it some more" "Yes! You do that. I would hate for him to ruin our day"

I can tell she was feeling very uneasy about him attending any of the ceremonies. That night after she excused herself and went back to bed, she laid there thinking how she is going to handle this. Carlton is a loose string and a possible threat to me or even her for that matter. She was also concerned about Cathy being locked away in the cellar. She had only left enough food to last about a year and it has been over a year and she was still alive. She thought she would be dead by now, but was somehow still hanging on. Then again, that was Cathy—A survivor!

The next morning at breakfast Clarice asked me "Son, are you sure about living at the old mansion?" "Yes mother. Helena and I will be very happy here. Besides I think father would have wanted it that way". She was pleased and nervous at the same time, and then she told me she was going to have more security put on the hotel for our safety.

I could tell something was still troubling her; and when I asked, "Are you okay?"

"I'm still feeling under the weather but I will soon be okay".

I kissed her on her forehead and said, "I am leaving to go to the office and will see you later this evening. Mother, please get back in bed and rest". "Frances, you are such a good son—I love you" "I love you too mother. Now go back to bed!"

We were a few days away before the grand opening, and each hour mother was getting more nervous and anxious because she felt Carlton was going to do something and not sure what. She realized she better move first. She had an detective check some things out about Carlton. She found out that he had a nervous breakdown, and was diagnosed with manic depression since his twin's alleged death. In addition, the record showed he had been hospitalized for suicide attempts.

One of the nurses stated that he dresses like his sister and hear her voice calling him. All this information had troubled Clarice as she realized this man has gone mad. She found out which hotel he was staying at by inquiring on the phone. Then she went to his hotel to stake him out personally, while the detective followed Carlton to the library. Her investigator told her he was researching her history. She soon realized that she was the target and not me. After going to the library and checking the sign in log, she saw he used the microfilm and assumed he was checking old news articles about her just like his sister. While mother was following his footsteps, she was being followed herself and not realizing it. Her investigator would report all of his whereabouts to her. She was so enthralled about getting Carlton that she was not paying attention of who was behind her. She went to his hotel and waited for the coast to be clear to try to enter his room, but his door was already opened because the cleaning lady had just entered his room. So, she took the door key off the cleaning cart to access his room later, once the cleaning lady was done. Mother was known for being quick, slick and able to get in and out of situations very swiftly.

After the maid got through changing sheets, making the bed and cleaning the bathroom she walked out of the room. Clarice went behind her and unlocked the door, then placed the key card on the floor outside the door to give the impression the maid had dropped it while leaving. Clarice knew she had to move quickly to find out what his plans were. She searched his drawers for any clues she could find and suitcase. When she opened his suitcase she found a gun and newspaper of the grand opening of the House of Elliott. Then the door was about to open so she hid in the closet. Sweating profusely and being almost caught, she made sure not to make a sound or move. She could not believe she was stuck in this predicament.

Carlton entered his room, sat on his bed, and made a phone call to check his voice mail messages. Clarice's heart was pounding as she feared he would open his closet door and see her standing there. Just then, his room phone rang and it was the desk clerk. She told him there was a gentleman at the front desk to see him. When he asked for his name, the clerk said the person refuses to give their name. He got up and left out of his room after going to the restroom. That is when Clarice dashed out of his room dropping her cell phone out of her purse, near the door inside the room.

When she got in her car and she drove straight to the mansion terrified that she had just made a narrow escape and did not accomplish anything. When she walked in the door her daughters were there with their husbands, which took her by surprise. She totally forgot that her daughters were arriving that day to prepare for the grand opening.

First thing Tranice said was "Mother, where were you? I have been calling and there was no answer!" Clarice told her daughter that her phone had been set to vibrate and that is why she did not answer. Lavern could tell something was wrong with her mother as she looked very distressed, hectic and had that nervous energy about her.

Tranice said, "Well, the grand opening is tomorrow and I would like to take a tour around the new place" Clarice told her "Very well. Let us go" Lavern asked "where is Frances?" And Clarice told her "At work dear, he will be here this evening". "He's working this late mother

"Lavern, please, I don't know your brother's whereabouts!" But Lavern knew something was terribly wrong because of how irritated she was. They proceeded with the tour of the new hotel.

After they had toured the hotel and settled in, I came walking in just in time for dinner. I was happy to see my sisters make it for the opening. At dinner, Tranice was going on as usual about work and then started to drill me about business and the reports while Lavern was looking at our mother like something was wrong. Clarice was troubled that Carlton was going to do something the next day and how she did not get to do anything to him. I could tell it was driving her crazy also.

Suddenly while having dessert, Tranice cell phone rang and mother thought it was hers so she went to look for her cell phone and could not find it. She almost turned ghost white when she realized she lost her phone. She excused herself and went outside, checked her car, and could not find it. She thought no way did she drop it at Carlton's hotel. Then, she remembered hearing something fall as she exited Carlton's room. When she walked back into the mansion, she looked at all three of us and fainted. "Oh my God . . . Did she drop dead?!" yelled Tranice while Lavern and I ran to her side.

I grabbed her before she hit the floor and her daughters were shocked because they never seen their mother pass out before. She became ill knowing that she may be heading for her demise. We all tried to console her and give her some tea but she was too distressed saying, "I'm going to die"

Tranice felt this whole hotel nonsense was just too much for her. While Lavern knew her mother was over her head in something. There was no fever and her mother is much too health conscience to be that physically ill. The question was—what did she get herself into this time? The girls got our mother into bed and she was frightened that any moment Carlton or the law was going to get her for breaking into his hotel room. Or even worse, that Carlton was going to kill her. Lavern stayed with mother that night and slept with her to make sure she was okay.

Chapter Eight

(Deadly Women)

Today was the big day, the grand opening of a hotel that should have taken place thirty years ago. My father Frances Elliott died too soon to see his vision come to life. Close friends, colleagues, and family were flying in, to be part of this celebration and to stay at the new hotel. All the hard work that mother and I had done and all the evil work as well.

Mother was staring out of the window thinking about her childhood. What her mother went through on the day she was exposed openly, and brought to a public shame and now her day had come. She felt Cathy would come back to bite her in the end. Not knowing where Carlton was or what he is going to do was tearing her up inside. But, she was going to face the music alone and with dignity like her mom did when she was a child. For her mother, it was a lighter that marked the end of her. As for Clarice, her mobile phone. As minutes turned into hours, the staff was getting ready as well as mother, and my sisters. Before the event started, she wanted to see the special guest list and saw Carlton's name on it. She was about to ask me why, however, she could not bring herself to ask. The festivities began at 7:00pm and it was a red carpet event. Everyone loved the new hotel and the amenities that came with it. Reporters came from everywhere. Clarice could not really enjoy herself because she kept waiting for Carlton to arrive or do something. Nevertheless, the night went on as planned. Finally, I wanted to thank some special people and started to name them one by one. She walked over to her daughters and held there hand, thinking this is it. But, when I got to Carlton's name and I wanted to thank my special friend for coming, he was not there.

Then, when I called Carlton's name again, one of the waiters walked up to me and handed me a note. Mother's heart was pounding and her daughter could feel their mother's pulse in their hand. I read the note silently to myself, and then I rubbed my hair back and had a strange look on my face. I shook my head no and looked directly at my mother. She was looking directly at me and was probably screaming on the inside, just dying with anticipation on what that note read. After I regrouped, I proceeded with thanking people. Everyone was feeling festive and having a wonderful time, drinking, mingling, and dancing. Then, I walked out on the terrace of the hotel and waited. As much as she wanted to walk up to me, she knew not to and played it cool. She never came outside to see what was going on.

The remainder of the night was a success and our guests were retiring to the rooms, while others were leaving to go to an after party Laverne had planned for our guest.

Mother went back to the old mansion and had a glass of wine waiting for me to come home. My fiancé and I walked in, I told her to go ahead, and I will follow her shortly. Then I walked over to my mother, put my arms around her tiny waist and handed her the note. She looked me in the eyes and slowly took the note and it read:

"It is with regret that your dear friend Carlton St. Claire had committed suicide by hanging in his hotel room"

She dropped the note, put her hand over her mouth, and had tears in her eyes. She said, "Son, I'm sorry about your friend" How could this be? Is what she thought. I sat next to her and kissed her cheek and said, "Good night mother, I'm turning in "Then just before walking off I stopped and said, "Oh, I think you were looking for this! "Then I handed her, her cell phone. She hugged me, cried, and said "I'm sorry" and I put my finger over her dainty lips and said,

"No mother, don't be sorry. Just know that I love you and would never allow anyone to harm you. Carlton was insane and going to kill you, and I would see him dead first."

She said, "How did you know my phone was there?" "While you were following Carlton, I was following you. Carlton became obsessed and blamed you for everything. Therefore, I had to take care of him. I was the gentlemen in the lobby" "But what about the investigator I had hired?" "I relieved him of his duty and paid him off" "You did this for me Frances?" "I would do anything for you mother to guarantee your safety and happiness. Now good night mother & I love you" With tears in her eyes, she walked up to me and kissed me and walked away.

A couple of days later, after my marriage to Helena, my mother decided to leave New York and move in with us. Everything was going well in our lives and we were more successful than ever. After Helena and I had been married now for a couple of weeks and back from our honeymoon, I wanted to celebrate mother moving in with us.

One day while mother and Helena went clothes shopping, I had decided to prepare dinner—lobster, rice pilaf, asparagus and garlic bread. Now, I needed the perfect wine to go with what I was preparing. I went to our cellar to find a vintage white wine. While trying to choose from our vast selection of red and white wine, I dropped a bottle and it burst. When I went to pick up the broken glasses, I noticed a hidden door behind the wine rack. As many times as I been to this cellar, I've never notice a door behind the rack of wine. I began to move the wine bottles slowly wondering why would there be a hidden door. By this time, mother and Helena were back from shopping.

As I moved all the bottles, I took a crow bar and began to jimmy the door apart until the lock broke. I opened it and walked into this hidden room, and there lying down on an old decrepit cot was Cathy. I stopped and stared as I could not believe what I was seeing. She was pale white, malnourished, thin and helpless looking. When she saw me, she got up slowly and ran over to me crying and saying

"Alex, I knew you would come and rescue me"—then she collapse in my arm, unconscious. I yelled for them upstairs to help me and sure enough mother came running quickly down the stairs and stopped dead in her tracks, as if she had seen a ghost. Almost the same reaction I had. I thought Cathy was a ghost until she fell into my arms.

"Mother, get a doctor quick" But she stood there in shock and could not move. Then Helena came downstairs and screamed!

I told my mother, who was just standing there, to hold Cathy while I get help. Then, I ran upstairs to call an ambulance. While Clarice was holding Cathy, she told Helena to get some water from upstairs and smelling sauce from the medicine cabinet. She was holding Cathy in her arms panicking and extremely frightened. Then, I came back down stairs and I took her out of Clarice embrace and was holding her close to my heart saying "My sweet Cathy" and begging her not to die. Shortly afterwards, the ambulance arrived and they tried to revive her, fearing she may had suffered a heart attack. But as it turned out, it was dehydration and shock. I rode in the ambulance with her while mother and Helena followed us in the limousine. I held Cathy hands and begged her to hang in there and don't die on me. Once we got to the emergency room she was immediately admitted and I.V. was given to her to bring her back out of state of unconscious. She slept the rest of the night and I stayed by her side. Mother tried to get me to leave, but I wasn't going anywhere.

"Frances, why don't you leave and I will stay watch over her" said mother. "There is no way I am leaving her and especially with you. Why was she in our cellar? And how long was she locked in there? Mother, you have some explaining to do" she then started to pace, rubbing her hands together in a nervous way. "Son, let me explain"

"Oh, you will have some explaining to do, but after she wakes" she just dropped her head and left. But she didn't go far; she was in the waiting room pacing back and forth and on her cell phone.

Cathy was out all night until the next morning before she came to, but extremely weak and barely able to speak. She looked at me with those beautiful blue eyes of hers and took my hand. She held it so gently and whispered "Thank you for getting me out of that horrible dungeon that I was locked away in" "Cathy, I am so sorry. I had no idea you were in there and that close to me. Can you ever forgive me for not getting to you sooner?" "I forgive you, my true love, I forgive you" as tears filled her eyes. "I know right now you are very weak, but please tell me what happened. How did you get in there? Was it my mother or the sheriff?"

She closed her eyes and turned her head away from me and said "I need to see Clarice" "Why? Why would you want to see her?"

"I need to talk to her Alex, where is she?" "I will have her to come here and see you" and then she nodded her head at me and drifted off to sleep.

Meanwhile, mother had gone into the cellar and inspected it and tried to hide whatever evidence she could. She noticed her old chest sitting in the corner, which had to be over 30 years old. She saw it had been pried open. In it was years of her intimate thoughts—her diary. There were several diaries in that chest from childhood to adulthood. It almost made her vomit, not knowing if Cathy had read her life's history. Incriminating things about her past and all the men she ever dealt with one way or the other. That morning, I called her. "Mother, I need you here at the hospital. Cathy would like to see you . . . alone" "Okay dear, I'm on my way"

As soon as my mother arrived, I looked at her with disgust and walked out of the room to give them privacy. Cathy had sat up in her bed waiting for her to walk in. "Cathy, you look so much better" "No thanks to you Clarice" "I know what I did was rather harsh and even demented. But please forgive me! I've never meant to do you any harm" "You left me to die in a decrepit and cold cellar, and yet you didn't mean to do me any harm? Surely, you can do better than that Clarice"

"I know you hate me Cathy, and I could not much blame you. But I was afraid of losing my son again to another woman. After that woman died who took him from me, I wanted him to myself. I wanted Frances to myself because he loved you too much and I feared losing him again" "You left me to die Clarice, and if Alex hadn't rescued me, I would have. You're a witch"

"Cathy, I'm sorry and at your mercy. Please don't turn me into the law or tell my son what I've done"

"As much as I despise you and would love to turn you in—I pity you. I pity all that you have gone through. That's right Clarice; I know all of your past and those you have hurt, even the darkest secrets. I know your mother abandoned you. You were born a bastard, sent to a boarding school where a priest tried to molest you. I know all about Frances Sr and your relationship with him. The men you were married to and murdered! The list is endless about how much I know about you. As beautiful as you think you are, you have such an ugly side. So you see, I pity and feel sorry for the miserable life you had" "Okay Cathy, since you know so much about me and my past, then you must know that if I wanted you dead you would be dead already. So what are you going to do with this information you have on me? Turn me in to the authorities or destroy my relationship with my only son?" "You know Clarice; it's not what I'm going to do to you. It's what you're going to do for me" "And what is that?" Cathy closed her eyes and smirked and opened them again and asked me to bow down and get on my knees. I looked hesitantly at first, because I had never bowed down to anyone. But now she had me backed into a corner, and I was at her mercy. So I did!

"I thought long and hard about this Clarice. Early this morning I was prepared to report you to the law and then I realized with all of your resource you would probably get off. But then there is your son, whom I'm sure by now you love. So, this is what I'm going to do. I'm not going to report you to the law or tell Alex that is was you—on one condition. First, you are going to pay me for keeping me locked up. In the amount one million pounds! Next, you are going to give me your blessings to marry your son—and get rid of his wife. It will be our little secret unless of course you want to write it down in your diary. Finally, you are going to add me as an heir to the House of Elliott giving me one quarter of your total assets, making me as equal as your daughters. How is that for revenge? Or you can go to trial and I will bring up the dead husbands as well as what you did to me."

My eyes sunk into my head and went from green to black. Bile had risen in my throat with the utmost hatred toward her. My lips tightened to a fine thin line and as my face turned red. Then I closed my eyes for a moment and said "Because of my son and I have done you wrong for no reason. I will comply with your many well thought out requests" "Very well Clarice, I will tell your son that the sheriff locked me away and not you. But first I want

to see everything in writing and this will be our secret."
"As you wish Cathy, I will have my attorney make the appropriate changes" Moments later Frances came back into the room and asked "Is everything okay, Cathy?"

"Yes my love. Your mother and I had some things to talk about, but she is leaving right now" I looked over at my mother and she put her hands on my shoulder and said "I'm sorry Cathy had suffered all these months in our cellar. I had no idea that the sheriff locked her away with very little food" I just stared at her and then glanced over to Cathy to confirm what she was telling me. And Cathy nodded her head yes to me. But I could feel the tension between the two of them. Mother had left and went to see her attorney and drew up a new will. I stayed with Cathy and told her all that had happened while we thought she was dead. The hardest part next to me being married, was telling her that Carlton had committed suicide. This broke her heart and she cried in my arms while I held her tightly.

"Alex, yesterday when you saved me there was a woman next to your mother. I can only presume she is your wife. When did you marry? Did you grieve for me at all?" I dropped my head in shame and said, "I married a couple of weeks ago. Cathy, I thought you were dead. I even made a memorial for you in our home town. Cathy, I love you and only want you. I only married her because I was grief stricken about you" "Nevertheless Alex, you are married"

And she slowly closed her eyes. I began to rub my head and said, "Cathy, I am going to annul my marriage with Helena. I can't bear losing you again. Please trust me my love—my marriage is over" tears filled her eyes and she hugged me. Then I asked her "Cathy, did my mother know you were in the cellar or have anything to do with you being there?"

"No my love, that is why I needed to talk to her first. It was the sheriff whom locked me in there" I looked at her, but deep down in my heart—I felt my dear sweet mother knew. But then again, I have lied to her about her brother. A couple of bold face liars is what we were, like mother—like son. I kissed her head and told her I would be back and had to take care of something. When I got home, Helena was sitting in the library by the fireplace drinking a glass of wine looking sad. I stood at the doorway looking at her and then she looked up at me and said, "She's going to be alright Frances?"

"Yes Helena, Cathy is doing well" "And she knows we are married?" I rubbed my face and walked over to her and sat down on the couch next to her. My heart dropped to my knees as this was more difficult than I thought. "Helena look, you know I love you and you are a good and sweet person" she sighed and looked away. "Let me guess Frances, you're going back to her? You are going to abandon your wife for a child hood crush?" "Helena, you know I love Cathy, and if I knew she was alive I would have never married."

"But you did Frances; you vowed until death do we part. There were no stipulations in that. You said 'death do we part'. Maybe I should hold you to that!"

I looked shocked because the sweet—genteel woman I knew would never talk this way to me. "I'm sorry Helena, but our marriage will be annulled and I do plan to marry Cathy. I never meant to hurt you and you will be taken good care of" I had no idea that mother was hiding behind the French doors listening to every word being said. Moments later, she came in with tea for all of us and asks to see me. I looked back at Helena while she was sipping her wine and walked over to mother and said, "Mother, now is not a good time"

"Son, I know you were in the middle of a heated conversation, but Helena is not going to let you go so easily without a fight or financial settlement and personally I don't want either."

"What do you suppose I do then?" At this point, I was very angry about this whole situation. "Son, I owe you a favor for what you did for me with Carlton. You don't want a scorned ex-wife in your life, while you start a new with Cathy. Do you?" "No I don't" "Then let me take care of this for you. A dead wife is always better than a scorned ex-wife", "Go and get some rest. I'll talk to Helena for you. I love you son" I sighed and hugged my mother and kissed her forehead and said, "I love you more" then I looked back towards the library, where Helena was sitting. I took my mother's advice and went upstairs to get some much needed rest. What I didn't know was that earlier that day my mother contacted her son in law Tony Luciano, and told him the situation about Cathy. How she was being blackmailed by her and wanted her dead. He assured Clarice that he would take care of this matter for her.

That night she stayed up with Helena comforting her and assuring her that everything will be fine. After chatting for a couple of hours, Helena joined me upstairs while Clarice sat in the library drinking her special tea. Moments later, Clarice phone rung and Tony said "It is done" mother closed her eyes in relief that Cathy was finally taken care of while in the hospital. Tony sent a hit man to the hospital to kill Cathy. He told Tony that he would put a non-traceable poison into her I.V. bag, giving the illusion of a heart attack.

The next morning while we were having breakfast, the phone rang. It was the hospital notifying me that Cathy had passed away from cardiac arrest. Again, my heart was crushed and I could not say one word. I just dropped the phone and wept. Mother looked at me with one eyebrow raised with curiosity. Helena walked over to me and consoled me, while I cried. My embrace was around her waist because I fell on my knees crying, as Helena and mother looked at each other with a devilish smirk on their faces—because, they won.

Again, I lost my beloved Cathy . . . the only woman who loved me, for me.

That's all . . . for now.

Frances Elliott